"PLUCK AND FIND."

"No," said Jennifer. She felt surprise at her resoluteness.

Without even seeming to hear her, the woman plucked the rose herself with a strangely mechanical motion. Immediately the red rose wilted in her hand, turning brown, then black in a shrunken corpse of its fragrant self. The spring at her feet abruptly dried up. Most surprising of all, the woman herself began to age before Jennifer's eyes. Her clear fair brow contracted in wrinkles, her nose grew knotted with hairs and warts, and her emerald eyes became dark and deep-sunken. Her back stooped, her hands shook with the tremor of palsy, and her crimson gown hung tattered and gray.

"Pluck and find," the old woman rasped. "Pluck and find the goddess within."

Other Avon Books by
Paul J. Willis

NO CLOCK IN THE FOREST

THE
STOLEN
RIVER

PAUL J. WILLIS

AVON BOOKS • NEW YORK

Thanks to Beth Scherfee for permission to print "Sierra Song" on page 119. All other borrowed poems in this book are taken from the public domain.

AVON BOOKS
A division of
The Hearst Corporation
1350 Avenue of the Americas
New York, New York 10019

Copyright © 1992 by Paul J. Willis
Cover art by Rowena Morrill
Map illustration by Laurie Vette
Published by arrangement with Crossway Books
Library of Congress Catalog Card Number: 92-5378
ISBN: 0-380-72080-9

First AvoNova Printing: December 1993

AVONOVA TRADEMARK REG. U.S. PAT. OFF. AND IN OTHER COUNTRIES, MARCA REGISTRADA, HECHO EN U.S.A.

Printed in the U.S.A.

RA 10 9 8 7 6 5 4 3 2 1

For my mother,
Earline Louise Willis

DOMI IN CORDE VALLIS

Paulina: It is required
You do awake your faith.

Shakespeare,
The Winter's Tale

E
N — S
W
a m o e n a s

Mirror Glacier

North Queen   Center Queen   South Queen

Nunatak

Chambers
Lake

Demaris
Cabin

Three Queens Wilderness

L. VETTE

River

Dark Divide

Semeas Gorge

To El Ai

Oak Grove

Tower of Otium

1

"READY WITH THE BOOK, JEN? I think I've got this thing." Ronald hovered over a thick yellow tripod, not looking at Jennifer but at a small bubble in a glass rod, part of a head-sized instrument that looked something like a green cyclops. He held out his arms on either side as if holding the instrument upright by a sorcery of air. Jennifer's father could level a theodolite in two minutes, even on ice, even in a wind. After ten weeks of practice it still took Ronald fifteen on a calm day.

What concerned him this morning was not the wind, for there was none, but the gray ceiling of lowering clouds. From where they stood on a rocky island dividing the glacier, they could no longer see the summit crest of the Center Queen above the cirque. Ronald knew that the glacier could be wrapped in fog in a matter of hours—minutes even. If he didn't complete his survey by then, he would have to start over another day. This late in the season, there would not be many good days left.

"Let's fake the data," Jennifer said as if reading his thoughts. "This glacier's been moving one foot a day all summer. It's not like it's going to change its ways this week or anything." She was lounging by a rock cairn on her olive rucksack, her parka hood pulled all the way about her face in the sunless chill.

"But—"

"Oh yes," said Jennifer, jumping up. "It's for *science!*" She

11

threw out her arms like a cheerleader, then regathered herself and demurely held an invisible microphone to her lips. "Ronald Miller, junior researcher, apprentice and pawn to the eminent, learned, world-renowned senior glaciologist Dr. Geoffrey Howe, Ph.D., here with us today on this barren nunatak separating the twin lobes of the Mirror Glacier high up in the unexplored reaches of the savage Three Queens Wilderness—here, I say, with his lovely assistant, Ms. Jennifer Howe, the beguiling daughter of the aforementioned Dr. Geoffrey. Yes, Ronald Miller, by his exacting persistence, here to discover what no man has found or known before (and what no woman would ever care to)—to probe before our very eyes this mystery of the universe, this question at the center of existence: *Do glaciers really move?*

"And the answer is—*yes*! The Everlasting Yea! Zounds! Zeus! Great Yin and Yang! A foot a day! Every day! All summer long! And the dedicated Mr. Miller is about to prove, after three more hours of freezing his scientific rear (not to mention the derriere of his lovely assistant), that this week too—wonder of wonders—the Mirror Glacier has moved *seven feet*! Just like the *last* ten weeks!" She then began to make trumpet noises, punching the air with both fists as she imitated the intrepid theme song of National Geographic TV specials.

Ronald had by now a very silly look on his face, which is just what Jennifer wanted to produce. It is always a pleasure to embarrass a person in the course of his duty.

When Jennifer had finished her instrumental prelude, Ronald swung the blank eye of his green cyclops to the higher western lobe of the glacier. If he could sight in all of the bright orange flags that were spaced in an arc across its width, he might have time to track the flags on the lower—and wider—eastern lobe. Jennifer stood resignedly beside him, holding a pencil and a bright yellow notebook that said on the cover, *Write in the Rain.*

"Okay," said Ronald, squinting through the scope. "First one, horizontal reading: 63 degrees, 24 minutes, 17 seconds."

Jennifer wrote down, "#1H: 63° 24' 17"," and then, "dried peas, bulgur, tuna, vanilla pudding." She knew that her father liked this combination and that Ronald didn't care. She wasn't sure about the others down in the cave and over on the North Queen. Being expedition cook—and logistics coordinator—wasn't easy.

Ronald shifted the scope slightly. "Number two, horizontal: 66 degrees, 49—"

"What do you think about Jakes—and Goober and Cheyenne and Maid Marian—think they'll go for that tuna thing again? And that strange fat fellow, Escee, it's hard to tell what he'd like at all. Roscoe, I know *he* won't eat it, but he won't eat anything. 'Steak,' he says, 'gimme steak, woman.' And I tell him, 'We just do veggies here, Roscoe, you know that—same as they did in the Garden of Eden.' And he says, 'Maybe that's why they call it the Fortunate Fall. Ha—ha—ha—ha.'" Jennifer put on a belly laugh to imitate the carnivorous Roscoe.

"Horizontal: 66, 49—"

"Ronald!"

"Jen!"

"I asked you a question, Mr. Science. Now give me some help on the old menu. You have no idea how hard it is to think of something every night."

"Tuna's fine," he said politely. He sighed and looked up. The clouds seemed closer.

She knew she could expect no more, and that she really should not have interrupted, but even so, Ronald drove her a little bit mad.

He located the next three flags, and Jennifer wrote down the coordinates. She was quiet until he started mumbling he couldn't find the sixth one. "The one below the icefall?" she offered. "Maybe something fell on it. And good riddance. One less piece of worthless data."

"What's that?" said Ronald.

"I said one less piece—"

"No . . . on the glacier. Something moving."

"Heavens. Run!" Jennifer cried. "Bigfoot! The Abominable Sasquatch! Maybe even a monstrous rosy finch, come to reclaim her rightful realm and peck out the eyes of peeping intruders. Or—Frankenstein! The monster, I mean, not the scientist—but hey, what's the difference? Ever read that book in Calculus, Ronald? About half the time he's cruising glaciers in Switzerland. Scary, huh? And all from the addled imagination of a nineteen-year-old child-bride cooped up in the Alps for a rainy summer with two of the most self-centered men in human intellectual history. Sound familiar? Not exactly, I know—I'm only a child-bride to be."

"I think it's a marmot," Ronald said matter-of-factly. "But I've never seen one this high. Look for yourself."

He stepped back, and Jennifer refocused the lens just in time to indeed catch sight of a hoary marmot. It loomed before her, bigger than she thought it could be, then disappeared into a dip of the glacier. For a moment she looked quite serious. Marmots, she knew, were the largest of North American rodents, but this one seemed much larger still. She was reminded of something rather odd that she had seen the night before, something she did not care to speak about.

"You see it then?" Ronald asked.

"Marmot ahoy!" She tossed back her hood. "Mr. Smee! Pipe up the crew! All hands on deck! Double the powder and shorten the fuse! Range 42. Elevation 65. Three degrees west. Steady now . . . steady . . ." She lit the breech of the theodolite and sent the echo of a cannonball roaring across the glacier.

"Blast it all!" she cried, swiveling the scope back into position. "We've missed the scurvy knave again."

"Careful with that," Ronald said quietly. "Don't yank it off level, Jen."

"But here," she said, peering in the glass and stepping back smugly, "we did locate your little flag, still gallantly streaming and all that. Just took a good bomb burst to find it, I guess."

He checked and nodded. "Hey, thanks."

"Hey, it was nothing."

To prove her congeniality she took down the next nine readings in silence. They made an unconsciously heroic pair, standing docilely side by side on a nub of talus halfway up the immense white flanks of a quiet volcano. The scissored bowl of the glacier before them was almost a mile across, extending from the clouds near the summit to the silvered fan of its terminus a good deal below them. There the glacier decayed beneath piles of boulders that merged with heather farther down near a large gray lake on a windswept pass. Beyond the lake another mountain, banded with crumbling lava cliffs, reached into the thick flat clouds.

The glacier behind them was even larger, falling down the northeast flank of the Center Queen to a river valley far below that curved into the east and south. This lobe splintered apart beneath its debris at an elevation where cedar and hemlock lined the banks. From the confusion of its end a shining rush of water emerged and lost itself in the dark forest.

As Ronald worked, measuring a baseline angle to each orange flag till he reached the one almost at his feet, the gray-bellied clouds sagged down from the summit and wisps of fog began to enshroud them. This last flag was firmly in view, and then it was not. He read off the degrees and minutes and seconds without being exactly sure the sights were fixed on the base of the staff.

"That's it," he said flatly. "We'll have to do the rest tomorrow." The fog then firmly closed in around them, a sudden and eternal cloak. Normally he would sight in again on the farthest flag to attain closure, checking to see if the instrument had in fact remained level, but of course he could not. This left his data sadly provisional, and left Ronald sadly distressed. What would Dr. Howe say? If Ronald had leveled the theodolite quickly at the start, there might have been time.

"Tomorrow?" said Jennifer. "Tomorrow's Sunday. Tomorrow's our day to hike down to the Demaris Cabin, remember? Gwen and William are expecting us. We get one day off a week, you know—you need to remember how to use it."

Unlike Jennifer, Ronald did not like to argue. He was silent for a lengthy moment, which bothered Jennifer more than anything. Then he said, "The weekly survey's got to be done, Jen. I can't help it. And the ablation stakes have to be measured too. There's just one week left before school starts, and still so much to do. Your father needs me down in the cave and I told him I'd be ready Monday."

It seemed they had had some version of this exchange all summer. Jennifer looked dispiritedly down through the fog as if searching for something new to say. And suddenly her eyes widened.

"Well, look who's here," she breathed. "The Elvis Presley of all marmots." She laughed as she said it but felt a hollow shudder inside. Creeping off the glacier and onto their nunatak forty feet below them, barely visible in the fog, was the out-sized marmot they had seen by flag number six on the icefall. It climbed the talus to where they stood and seated itself upright on a rock as if it were the overseer of their joint enterprise.

"Scat," said Jennifer. "Scram! Beat it! Don't come where you're not wanted. You're interfering with the important work of the GNP, the prestigious Glacier and Nature Project, and are liable to censure for obstructing research, for just being, for using these few moments of life to sit there on that old gray stone. Up! up! my friend—you know the rest."

The marmot stayed put and looked at her with incurious eyes. It was so obese, so absolutely dropsical, that she could have thought it a misshapen bear cub. She wondered how it moved at all.

"Ignore him," said Ronald. "He'll go away." He unscrewed the theodolite from its base, stowed it away, and strapped the legs of the tripod together.

Jennifer looked hard at the marmot. Its eyes seemed dead. "Like yeah," she said. "Like let's ignore the Statue of Liberty." She pulled her crampons out of her rucksack and plucked off the rubber spiders protecting the prongs. She strapped them on the bottom of her boots and had already tied the rope to her harness when Ronald finally found his crampons underneath the theodolite case. He was so slow, so deliberate in everything he did. Each day it seemed to arouse her impatience a little more. She started down to the edge of the glacier they'd just surveyed to hurry him up, to brood alone, and perhaps to escape the presence of the marmot.

"Don't go on the glacier till I can belay you," Ronald called after her.

Jennifer huffed. It was like being told not to cross the street, something that did not bear repeating. She clashed down stone and scree in her crampons, pulling loops of rope behind her, and stopped beside a pillar of rock at the frozen shore. The fog had thickened, and already Ronald was lost from view.

The snow before her was hard-packed firn, the stubborn remnant of late September. A bit lower, there would be none at all, just bare ice littered with rock and grime. Sixty feet down the slope of firn, past a bamboo wand they had left to mark the proper path, lay a gaping bergschrund—a crevasse along the edge of the glacier that separated the moving ice from the more immobile snow by the nunatak. She could not see the crevasse in the fog, but she could hear the lonely gurgle of meltwater trickling away in its icy depths. When Ronald joined her, he would belay the rope from the pillar of rock until she was safely across the schrund on a sunken snowbridge.

When they had come in early July to lay out the flags and survey stations, the crevasse had been merely a hairline crack. Two weeks later Jennifer had punched through to her waist, and Ronald, behind her, had anchored the rope to his ax in the snow as she struggled out, lest the entire roof collapse and she with it. By late August the bergschrund was twelve feet wide and numberless deep, and they crossed on a bridge that week by week sagged lower in the center, so that recently they did not so much balance across it as descend to the middle and climb up the other side.

Ronald crashed down out of the fog and looped a sling on the pedestal. He rubbed her nose with an outstretched finger. "Glob of sunscreen there," he said. "Belay's on."

2

RONALD AND JENNIFER did not descend below the fog till the firn gave out and their crampons bit into steely ice near the snout of the glacier. This was fortunate, for the wands they followed out of the cloud had weeks ago melted out and fallen down on the bare ice. Roped together they threaded their way, Jennifer first, down gray frozen ramps past sharp chasms of deep blue—the true color of the heart of a glacier—to a steep incline that left them among a wasteland of boulders at glacier's end.

The ice they had left rose up at their backs in a furrowed wall, and the heaps of rocks lay spread out before them to a long ridged mound—a terminal moraine—fencing them into a large enclosure. The moraine was breached by a small stream which issued from a cave in the ice nearby. They were taking off crampons and coiling the rope when a tall man in an orange parka stepped out of the black hole. He was talking into a radio, and his face beamed with the satisfied intensity of work worth doing. After a brief exchange about something with someone, he collapsed the antenna and caught their eye.

"Well!" he said, and walked firmly toward them. "You're getting on as a surveyor, Ronald. Finished early this time, eh? Fine, fine." His rather red face bobbed up and down with hearty approval. "Just in time. We can use you in here. Dr. Slupensky has just located a major reservoir under the cirque of the eastern lobe. The largest I've seen *anywhere*. We have to sound it, of course, and it's opened a whole new down-glacial system to map before the end of the season."

Ronald started to answer, but the man cut him off. "Jennifer, how's my girl?"

"Fine, Dad. Tuna tonight?" Seeing him, she wished her mother were there to make it.

"It's foggy, Dr. Howe," Ronald got in. "We didn't finish." He didn't say that as far as the data were concerned, they hadn't really gotten started.

Jennifer's father scratched the silver stubble on his chin. "That so," he said, looking up at the low dark clouds. "Well, it can't be helped. Get in here with us for the afternoon and you can finish topside tomorrow perhaps."

"Tomorrow?" said Jennifer.

Her father went on undeflected. "Jennifer, down you go. Be time to think of supper soon, and anyway, I have a message for you to give to our visitor in camp. I came out to raise him on the radio, but he must have forgotten the schedule. Tell him we found the sub-glacial lake. That'll make him happy."

Before he had finished, Jennifer was returning the wave of two figures who had appeared in the gateway of the moraine. "Gwen!" she shouted. A genuine smile came to her lips. "William!"

"Well," said her father, playing as ever the sanguine host, "look who's here—our loyal greenclads!" He advanced down the small stream to meet them walking up. The woman wore the khaki shirt and dark green pants of the Forest Service, not pressed and trim in a rangerly way, but several sizes larger than seemed to be necessary. She had an open face and thick blonde braids, the sort Jennifer envied against her thin disheveled chestnut hair. Behind her came a strong-built man with a profoundly humble look on his face that belied the shadow of bristle on his chin. He carried a wooden-shafted ax much longer than the metallic ones beside Ronald and Jennifer.

Dr. Howe shook the hands of the new arrivals cordially, still saying, "Well, well." Jennifer caught up to her father and gave both of them hugs, and Ronald did something—not quite a handshake, not quite a hug—awkwardly in between. With friendly vigor they talked about the chances of rain and their states of health and the glacial progress of research. Then Dr. Howe asked, "To what do we owe the honor of your presence? Just visiting, or . . . ?"

"Actually," said the woman named Gwen, "we noticed the helicopter that flew in yesterday afternoon, and since your landing pad was only constructed for emergency use, by terms of your special use permit, we wondered if you had run into trouble. We couldn't get you on the two-way radio, so we thought we'd hike up ourselves and check."

"Yes, yes," said Dr. Howe to the rocks at his feet. "Your concern much appreciated. No mishaps, we're all fine, just the advent of a special visitor, that's all. Our grant sponsor—needed to check on the project and such. A bit in a hurry, no time to walk—I believe, my dear, he worked things out with your district supervisor—a little exception. For science, you know."

There was an awkward pause.

"But no one is authorized to make that exception," Gwen said firmly. William touched her arm in caution. "I don't know what the super may have done at the office, but here on site I have to consider that helicopter an illegal intrusion. As you well know, no motorized vehicles or motorized equipment of any kind are allowed within a wilderness area. Federal law. I'm sorry, Dr. Howe, and no offense, but I'll have to find your visitor and write out a violation."

"Great!" said Jennifer. "Just where I'm headed. We can go together." She knew this was an impertinence, but it was the way she really felt, and she thought to interpose a little ease before her father became upset.

At present he was sputtering in a gentlemanly sort of way, still the master of ceremonies. "Now, now, now, Gwen dear, you understand I completely admire your adherence to duty—quite exemplary, to be sure—but I don't know if our visitor would take your perfectly justified remonstrances in quite the way you intend them. Escee is very much the important man, not used to much in the way of criticism—I'm not sure it would do to call his attention to his mode of travel just now, what with our research just reaching a critical stage. Perhaps a discreet letter addressed to his secretary—I'll vouch they'd be happy to pay the fine, if there is one for this sort of thing. Just a friendly note of caution—your best interests in mind, of course. I'm sure he'd be willing to put in a little word for you at the district headquarters, and—"

"Dr. Howe!" said Gwen, her face flushed. "Do you realize what you just—"

"Now, now, now, Gwen dear, I know what you're thinking. You're a few years older than Jennifer, and remarkably mature and perceptive, but you're still young, and with a little one on the way, I hear—" He winked and nodded grotesquely at William. "You and William need to be thinking about the future. A backcountry job at a wilderness cabin is all very well for a fit young couple like the two of you, but there are other positions available, promotions to be had, just the thing for a growing family and all that."

Jennifer was acutely embarrassed for her father. By the studied silence in Gwen's face she knew her friend was deeply offended.

"We appreciate your concern, Dr. Howe," William said huskily. He seemed uncertain how to navigate between elder and wife. "But—"

"But we're not for sale," Gwen said acidly.

Dr. Howe looked disconcerted, as if she had deliberately smashed his most expensive theodolite. Then his tension seemed to dissolve. "Of course you're not," he said warmly. "And I never meant to—"

"And where we raise our children is our business, Dr. Howe. I can think of many less healthy places than right here. In fact, I can't think of a healthier place than right here."

"As you wish, then, as you wish—didn't mean to intrude. Your domestic matters are no affair of mine, you're perfectly right, Gwen dear. Just trying to help."

"Do you want to help me right now then, by giving me the name of your guest?" She shed her rucksack and fished out an official-looking pad. "In case I can't find him?"

Dr. Howe looked rather flummoxed. "Gwen dear, if you feel you really need to do this, perhaps you could just leave the papers with us. Be glad to pass them on—at an opportune time."

William looked rather hopefully at Gwen.

"What ho!" said Dr. Howe. "Speak of the devil!" He was looking beyond them down the stream to the gap in the moraine whence Gwen and William had just come. Lumbering towards them over the stones was a bald-headed man in an ill-fitting crimson parka—ill-fitting because of the man's enormous bulk. He looked to Jennifer as if he might have rolled up the hill, and that if he rolled back down his case would be that of Humpty Dumpty's. As he jolted closer over the rocks, the deep tan of his face became apparent, as did the many furrows that began at his eyebrows and climaxed somewhere high atop his bare skull.

"Afternoon, Escee! We didn't expect you. Welcome to our laboratory." Dr. Howe genially swept his arms in every direction.

The man he called Escee labored toward them without any acknowledgment of the greeting. Before he quite reached

where they stood, he collapsed in a decided heap, resting on
his ample haunches until the others migrated into his presence. He was wheezing and puffing dramatically.

"That cursed hill. You never told me your cave was on top
of a mountain, Howe. Oh, for a drink."

Gwen pointed helpfully at the stream, but he didn't seem
to notice.

"But now that you're here," said Dr. Howe eagerly—"and
what a splendid surprise—we can give you a little tour, Escee."

"Sir," said Gwen, not even waiting to be introduced. "Sir?
Are you the one who—"

"Yes, yes," Dr. Howe interrupted, "precisely the one I've
been telling you about. Executive Director of Southland Hydro
Replenishment Research, here to visit one of the many projects
he and his group are so generously funding. Such a privilege
for—"

The man cut him off with a wave of his hand. "Just show
me the cave, Howe. And get me a drink."

"I've got something," Ronald volunteered. He jogged up
the stones to his pack for a poly bottle of lemonade.

"It's in mine," Jennifer called after him. "In the pocket next
to the data book."

Ronald returned with the lemonade and handed it to
Escee, who took it without any thanks and made a face as he
put the bottle to his lips.

Ronald was worried, but not by the man's response.
"Jennifer," he whispered, nudging her aside. "The data book. It
wasn't there." It held his entire summer's work, some but not
all of it copied into a ledger at basecamp. Just that morning he
had found the ledger shredded and chewed—by mice, he supposed.

"Must've dropped it into the schrund," she said. "You know,
accidentally." She snickered, then stopped. Her face registered
the certain pain of sudden recollection. "Oh , Ronald," she said.

"I left it. I know I did. I'm so sorry. It's just that that marmot—" She stopped and they looked at each other intently.

"We're ready then?" said Dr. Howe. "Ronald, will you join us? And, Jennifer, perhaps you could loan your ax and crampons to our—"

"I'm sorry, sir," Ronald mumbled.

"Eh, what's that?"

"I'm sorry, sir, but I can't go. I left the data book on the nunatak. After what happened to the ledger last night, I'd better go get it."

Escee finished the distasteful bottle of lemonade and rolled his eyes. "I see you run a tight ship here, Howe."

Jennifer's father visibly cringed, and Jennifer herself felt a sudden urge to tip the fat man into the stream. She saw Gwen sink onto a nearby boulder, suddenly pale.

"Gwen," she whispered, "you alright? You need to go down?"

"Sick," hissed Gwen. "I'm sick. We're all sick. The whole thing's sick."

Jennifer looked puzzled.

"The baby, I mean—that's all. No, that's not all. I can't stand it."

She stood up uneasily and addressed Escee. "Sir," she said, "if you are the one who flew in on the helicopter yesterday it is my duty to—" And here, as if it *were* her duty, Gwen suddenly and forcefully threw up on the stones that separated her from the rotund man. A little of it splashed on his boots, and he pulled them away in plain disgust.

William immediately began helping Gwen sit down again. "Take it easy," he said. "Just rest. We'll get back down nice and slow." To Dr. Howe he said apologetically, "I told her she wasn't up to this."

Jennifer touched William's shoulder. "Let me stay with her," she urged. "I've got to go down anyway, and Ronald needs someone to climb back up the glacier with him." She saw this as an opportunity for Ronald to spend time with a man she considered to be a model husband. Besides, she couldn't face the thought of Ronald's resentment quivering at the end of the rope as they climbed the two long hours to the data book—if indeed it was still there.

William checked Gwen's face. She nodded approval, and he turned to Ronald. "Alright with you?"

"Great," said Ronald, but it just sounded like "O.K." He was none too proud of the occasion.

"Well then, Gwen dear, we'll be seeing you," said Dr. Howe, helping Escee to his feet. "Do take care. You've got a little one to think of, you know—don't overdo it." He escorted the unsteady man to the entrance of the cave, where he commenced a lecture on recrystallization of glacial ice to apparently less than enraptured ears.

Ronald began uncoiling the rope, and he and William offered their good-byes to the women, William's heartfelt, Ronald's more tepid.

"Watch out for that man-eating marmot!" called Jennifer. It was a joke that she and Ronald shared from years ago when they had first met. Except now it felt forced.

"The what?" said William. He looked vaguely concerned and swung the pick of his ax to the ice as if testing its strength after long years of disuse.

3

WITH A LITTLE PERSUADING of her friend, Jennifer was able to strap Gwen's rucksack atop her own, and the two headed slowly down the stream. Once they had passed through a maze of moraines the rocks gave way to a smooth slope of dark green heather, broken by a narrow footpath stooping down in clay steps. The little stream occasionally stopped in small clear pools that were edged with the tawny grass of autumn. At one of these pools, perhaps halfway down to the lake below, Gwen asked to rest, and they stretched themselves on the brittle remnants of sunburnt stubble, watching the gray-bellied clouds sweep past.

They remained quiet for a long time. Gwen had a calm about her that seemed to Jennifer different from her own brooding silence. Jennifer was deciding whether to tell Gwen about the dream she had had the night before and what she had seen upon waking from it. Jennifer had gotten into her sleeping bag a bit late. The estimable Escee had suddenly arrived in late afternoon, and Jennifer at her father's bidding had prepared her best raisin and rice casserole, with onion bagels and some carefully saved cream cheese. The visitor ate it with grotesque scowls and grimaces which he did not even deign to aim in her direction, and after clean-up Jennifer left the cooking tent in a sour mood. In the starlight she strolled away from the camp to the edge of the lake, just where the outlet purled away from the quiet waters. She thought about

Ronald, back in camp and still earnestly listening with the others to the talk between her father and the visitor. She thought of returning to college in a week, and whether she should tell Dr. Hessler what she really thought of him and his precious English major. (Dr. Hessler's favorite word was *scholarly*, though *squalorly* was the way he said it.) And she thought of her present self, somehow broken like the stars in the water, her summer hopes not at all turning out the bright best way.

She walked back to her tent, a small dome-like affair, and crawled into her bag with the door left open, zipped down like a drawbridge to let in the freshness of the night. Immediately she fell asleep and dreamed herself lost in an angular maze of trimmed hedges, the sort she had once or twice explored in the formal gardens of an old brick mansion she had visited as a girl with her father soon after her mother had died. The hedge in her dream was thick and thorny and higher than her head, and the path kept turning in sharp corners until she arrived in an opening at the very center of the maze. Here there was a fountain of water—not a spigot on a pipe but a real spring bubbling out of the grass. Above the fountain a scarlet rose grew out of the hedge. Beside it stood a splendid woman dressed in red, with raven hair and clear green eyes. She was looking at Jennifer with an intensity that broke all bonds, and pointed to the scarlet rose. "Pluck and find the goddess within," the woman said in a deep clear voice. "Pluck and find."

Jennifer felt very frightened—the way she had when her mother had died—but she wanted to do what the woman had said. It felt necessary, and daring, and important—the path into her real future. Hardly taking her eyes from the eyes of the woman, she reached her hand to the stem of the rose and inadvertently pricked her finger on a thorn. "No!" she cried, and found herself awake. She felt her finger damp with blood outside her bag, and wondered if she had sliced it with the jag of a nail or the cusp of the zipper. The moon was up, shining in the open door, and the skin of her tent was all aglow. And there in the doorway, just at her feet, was the bloated marmot.

It sat fully erect, looking at her with dark dull eyes. She tried to scream, but no sound came. The marmot kept watch impassively, billowing mounds of fur and flesh inert in the moonlight, and in a few moments her fear changed to powerful disgust. She coiled her legs and kicked at him with her sleeping bag, and very slowly, as if not at all in response to her movement, he got down on all fours and walked away into the night.

On the glacier that day she had wanted to tell Ronald, especially when they had seen the marmot out on the ice, and even more when it came to them on the nunatak. But a dream—so silly—he wouldn't have listened. Now as she lay on her back by the stream, nursing her finger between her lips, she wanted even more to tell Gwen. But when she opened her mouth she heard herself asking, "Gwen, are you happy?"

Gwen looked bemused. "Sick, yes. Angry, yes. Happy?" She paused. "Yes."

"William is good to you, isn't he? I can tell."

"Well, yes. I think I'd say so. He's learning—and so am I."

"You mean, he wasn't always? Was he selfish at first? Or, I mean, insensitive?"

Gwen laughed weakly. "When we first met he was just bashful, that's all. An old friend brought him by the cabin one evening, and they stayed the night. He was so sure we had met before, and it embarrassed him to say it—more when I assured him we were strangers, but hoped we could be better friends.

"How can I explain? He loved the country, just like me—not the flag *per se*, but the land itself. He liked what I did and asked what he could do to help. I could tell that he liked me, too, but it wasn't just a come-on. I got a lot of guys stopping by back then—you know, You-Can-Do-It Expedition types—I could tell *they* liked me. But William liked what I stood for—one creation, indivisible. He knew. Not for very long, he hadn't, but he knew.

"He had to go the next day, but he kept showing up on the weekends to climb. Funny, every weekend the rest of that summer it rained—hard. We did a lot of talking. In October our friend married us—in the presence of about one hundred marmots. For some reason, they all seemed interested."

"Sometimes they do," Jennifer put in.

"That was—let's see—six years ago now. Our anniversary is in just eight days."

"Six years," said Jennifer. "Maybe I told you that that's when Ronald and I met. Led, no doubt, by one of your suitors on You-Can-Do-It." She paused and laughed at the possibility. "I think he might have even taken us to your cabin. A woman gave us blueberries—maybe it was you."

Gwen smiled and shrugged. "Time goes by," she said.

"He—Ronald—was so cute then. Such a nerd. Even his name—he always had to go by *Ronald*. He was proud of it. I mean—*Ronald*! As if he were a fast-food clown or an aging actor. He wore these black nylon glasses like those old pictures of Buddy Holly. He was so pathetic I couldn't help liking him, even though he was two years younger—that matters in high school. We ended up at the same college, where Dad teaches. By then I had taken a couple years off—you know, to travel—but mostly I worked in a health food store right next to campus. So when Ronald came we were both freshmen. He took all of Dad's geology courses in the next two years—even one for graduate students. Meanwhile, I barely got by in Victorian lit and Renaissance poetry. I liked the readings in the health store better—these *wonderful* women reciting their stuff on, you know, the earth goddess and everything."

Gwen looked at her quizzically.

"From the heart, you knew it—it was *so* natural. But I could never get Ronald to come—he was always in the lab.

Which, well, has been the story, especially since we got engaged this spring. Dad thought he was doing us a favor to have me along as part of the research project this summer, since Ronald was coming anyway. But Ronald's been so—so *dedicated* up here. I hardly feel like I exist."

She half sat up and looked moodily out at the lake below and at the small bright puddle of tents on the shore. "We came here on that expedition six years back—just over that rise from the east. We weren't even sure it was the right lake. Except Ronald was sure. At the time I thought it was charming, the way he knew, forging ahead and not listening to anyone."

"William can be like that," said Gwen.

"Charming?"

"No—well, yes, of course, but—*focused*. Like I said, however, he's learning. When you love, he can learn."

It took Jennifer half a second before she realized she had been handed a piece of advice. She resented it, a little.

A raindrop fell, and Gwen suggested they go on. When the slope eased, they walked in the heather side by side, and Jennifer resumed their talk on safer ground. "The helicopter—that bothers you, doesn't it? And Escee—what a jerk. You've got to keep the rules, because that's your job, but they don't make it easy for you."

"It's more than all that," Gwen said wearily. "You know what your father's research is for, don't you?"

"For *science*," Jennifer announced. "To push back the frontiers of knowledge and benefit the future of man."

"That's all he told you?"

"He didn't have to, I already knew—since I was two, I think."

"Your father," said Gwen, "is interested in more than how fast these glaciers move and melt and how much water they discharge. At least, the people who are paying him—Escee—are not interested in these things for their own sake. But they are the kinds of things one needs to know if one is planning to build a dam downstream, say across the mouth of the Amoenas Gorge, forty miles below the glacier."

Jennifer received the information blandly. "Well, yes, I guess they were talking something about that last night. But Amoenas Gorge—that's way out of your district, right? A dam there is not going to interfere with *your* mountains, is it?"

"The gorge is part of the Three Queens Wilderness," Gwen said. "It may be forty miles downstream, but the river wraps around the peaks so that the damsite, at Otium, is but a little ways from the South Queen. But that part—the illegality—is literally neither here nor there. If you had once visited, you would feel—" She lapsed into silence, not knowing how to name the feeling.

"I'm sure it's very beautiful," Jennifer offered, feeling a bit uncomfortable in the face of Gwen's obvious emotion. When she said this, however, she was thinking how tired she was of the mountains, and how good it smelled—the herbs, the candles, the aromatic soaps—in the health food store. Perhaps she would not re-enroll in classes after all.

"It's not a matter of rules," said Gwen. "It's a matter of love."

Once again Jennifer sensed she was being corrected, and did not like it. By now they were getting close to the camp, a scattering of chartreuse tents near the shore of the lake. The clouds were lower and darker now in the late afternoon; the moraines behind them were lost to view, and the North Queen before them was likewise gone. Their world was merely a bowl of heather sloping down to the gray-flung lake.

Jennifer was in no hurry to get back. The thought of preparing another meal in the empty mess tent—prying open the lids of the large stack of tins—made her quite as nauseous in imagination as Gwen was in fact.

"I'm glad we're close," Gwen murmured. "I'm afraid I have to lie down again."

"Then use my tent," Jennifer said. "You know the one. I think I'll take a walk by the lake and then get supper started. There's still time. You rest until the others get back, and then you and William can eat with us."

Gwen agreed, and the two women parted beside the tent at the outskirts of camp. Jennifer left the rucksacks with Gwen, taking only her green cagoule in case the rain should begin in earnest. She began on a path heading counterclockwise about the lake, and was considering whether she should have returned to change out of her heavy boots when she saw something atop a rise set back from the water. It was only a ragged protuberance, really, a natural row of stones perhaps, but as she had never explored that spot before, and as the lapping of the water depressed her spirits, just as it had the night before, she sauntered away from the path by the shore to investigate. Some hundred yards brought her to a flat crest, and there on the heather was not simply a row of stones, but an entire enclosure, knee-high, of rocks fitted closely together. It looked for all the world like the old foundation of a cottage or cabin that might have once stood on this heathery knoll above the lake.

Jennifer saw all this in an instant. What drew her attention was not the stone remains, however, but something inside them. Planted erect in the rust-brown grass at the very center of the ruin was an old wooden ice ax, not quite as long as the one that William had carried with him to the glacier.

Jennifer stepped over the stones and onto the grass, and approached the ice ax gingerly as if making her way to a tombstone and fearing to walk atop the dead. When she reached the ax, her breath came in a sudden gasp. The shaft was weathered by rain, wind and snow into grainy ridges—but it was not that. The pick and the adze on the head of the ax were spotted with rust—but it was not that. What she saw, hidden from her heretofore since it bloomed on the south-facing side of the shaft, was a red, red rose, perfect in shape, growing out of the ax itself. Its little stem was grafted into the wood of the ax at the top of the shaft just under the pick and adze—not grafted but growing, as if roses naturally came from axes. In spite of the cloudiness of the day the flower was opened in full display, the soft layers of twining petals already dewed by the coming fog.

She knelt in wonder, not daring to touch the ax or its flower, and gazed for a long, long time. The clouds crept down, and the fog slipped round her without her knowing it, and still she gazed.

Then she heard a voice—whether in the fog or in her mind or in the memory of her dream she could not tell—but the voice told her, low and deep in full rich tones of womanhood, "Pluck and find the goddess within. Pluck and find."

At the sound of these words there welled up within her distaste for Ronald, disgust with her father, and poisonous envy for William and Gwen. Here was an action, a self, that would satisfy. As if in a trance, Jennifer reached her trembling fingers to the fragile stem. This time there was no thorn. The rose broke easily in her grasp, and she brought it hungrily to her face, crushing it to her nose and lips and closing her eyes in a fragrance she had never known.

She had only a moment to revel in the sweet sensation before she realized her fingers were wet. She pulled the rose away from her face, opened her eyes, and saw to her astonishment that her hands were dripping with crimson blood. Jennifer dropped the rose in horror and saw that the blood was not confined to her own hands but was also welling from the broken stem and streaking the wooden shaft to the ground.

"Stop!" she cried. "Oh, stop!" She wiped her hands on the dead grass and pressed her palms on the wounded shaft, applying the proper direct pressure as she had been taught in her first aid classes. But the blood kept rising through her fingers, and the wind blew past her in a mortal sigh. Her hands were crimson once again, and the entire shaft was coated with blood, collecting now in an outspreading stain on the ground that began to envelop the soles of her boots.

"Please, stop!" she cried in the rising wind. In desperation she let go the shaft and put her hands to the pick and the adze, gripping them hard against the slipperiness of her flesh. She screamed without words. In one mighty pull the ax was uprooted. And the bleeding stopped.

In that moment the rain began. What Jennifer realized, as she stood there gasping with the ice ax dangling in her hands, was that she heard it beating on a roof.

4

IT TOOK MOST of Ronald's concentration to follow the cleated holes in the ice that he and Jennifer had punched that morning with their crampons. In the fog there would not be much else to guide him until they got to last year's snow—the softer firn—which still held the wands upright. He was glad that William was well behind him. Ronald didn't feel like talking, and telegraphed as much by the rope that sawed between them across the ice.

He had met this quiet, steady man on a couple of occasions when Jennifer had taken him on their days off to the cabin where Gwen and William lived. It was three miles on a faint track down the outlet stream from Chambers Lake, then three miles more on a real trail down gentle switchbacks to where the cabin stood in the meadows and groves of timberline on the western flank of the Center Queen. It was a pleasant enough walk, and a fine thing, near the cabin, to stroll in the shade of real trees after days in the open on ice and heather.

Ronald remembered coming there for the first time six years before as a negligible member of a You-Can-Do-It Expedition, the trip on which he and Jennifer had met. A hailstorm had quite literally brought them together beneath an unpitched, crowded fly, and the tyrannies of their red-bearded leader had kept them from drifting apart. He recalled the strange eagerness with which the leader had allowed them to stop at the cabin for lunch, and how hot it was that midsummer day, and how cool it was when the ranger had invited them inside the basalt block walls into dim shade, and how they sat round a rough-hewn table and passed a bowl full of huckleberries that she had picked. He remembered too the crush of the berries on his dust-coated teeth, and some of the things that the backcountry ranger had explained to them about the Three Queens Wilderness—plans in the making for a ski resort on the South Queen, for geothermal drilling at timberline throughout the area, for clearcutting and new roads in the forest approaches to the peaks, and for a new dam on the nearby Amoenas Gorge. The ranger had sounded sarcastic as she told them these things—almost as if she didn't approve of them.

Which confused Ronald. He knew that God had made the world—all of creation—for Adam and Eve to subdue and have dominion over. What good was a wilderness locked up from human use? His geology classes with Dr. Howe had recently made him not so sure that God had created the earth, or that there really had been an Adam and Eve, but Ronald kept quiet about these doubts, and at any rate, he and his teacher were in perfect agreement that the earth was a storehouse of rich resources to be used for the benefit of humankind. Geologists helped uncover these riches and make them available for all. He thought of himself on this his first research expedition as one of a team of daring philanthropists, as a modern Prometheus of sorts, though in this instance he was helping to bring not fire but water.

He had guessed long ago that their purpose in measuring movement and wastage of glaciers on the east side of the Three Queens was to check their potential for water release to a downstream dam. Not only potential but also reliability. Occasionally scientists came across a glacier that "galloped," and signs were that the east lobe of the Mirror Glacier, the major source of the Amoenas River, had moved rather quickly at times in its history—much faster than the rather sedate one foot a day observed by the western lobe of the Mirror. In the ten weeks he had measured it, the eastern lobe had picked up speed to almost five feet *per diem*. Some glaciers could hit seventy, and when that happened, a glacier would literally explode, suddenly discharging giant volumes of water downstream. He had seen slides of Russian scientists fleeing what looked like part eruption and part tidal wave somewhere in the Pamirs. These glacial catastrophes happened much more frequently in volcanic regions, where sub-glacial warming could lubricate the underside of the glacier ice with unusual amounts of meltwater. The eastern lobe of the Mirror Glacier seemed to be sited on such a hot spot. This would account for the rather constant year-round outflow of water from the terminus. It would also account for the large sub-glacial reservoir discovered that day, the presence of which might please their visiting grant sponsor if he were ignorant of what it implied about this glacier's destructive potential. In Iceland they had a name for it: glacier burst. *Jokulhlaup*.

The point was, no dam could survive such a high-speed wall of ice and water. But people were eager to build this dam, and Dr. Howe, he could tell, was eager to please both them and their money. It was doubtful whether the good professor, now guiding his visitor through the caves that linked the two lobes, was at this very moment lecturing him on glacier surge and glacier burst. Not that Dr. Howe would suppress the evidence in his report. He simply might omit to interpret it, leaving it to engineers raised in the desert to draw their own desired conclusions from his glacial mass of glacial data.

These suspicions left Ronald with an ethical dilemma. In the last day or so, he had sometimes thought he should take the detestable Escee aside and apprise him of the real possibilities. On the other hand, he knew how rare an occurrence a *jokulhlaup* really was, especially in smaller glaciers in the middle latitudes, a point on which Dr. Howe kept insisting. Five feet a day was not unheard of for an alpine glacier, and the geologic evidence of a glacial catastrophe here in the past was rather vague. And the dam was needed. Great cities far to the south were dying of thirst.

Part of Ronald would have liked to talk about these things with William as they climbed. But he already knew, by a few hints the other had dropped, that William was definitely not in favor of any dam at all. Telling him about *jokulhlaups* would give him the ammunition he needed to alert the press, hire a lawyer, and stop the project altogether. And William would do it. Hadn't he stopped the ski resort, the geothermal drilling, the illegal clearcutting in just the same way in the past few years? The man was a fanatic, an archdruid if there ever was one. Quiet enough, pleasant enough, but a dangerous fanatic nonetheless.

When they first met, earlier in the summer, Ronald had been interested to learn that William was a computer programmer before he was married. Ronald had a fascination with computers himself. He looked forward to the moments, perhaps next month, when he would transform the data he had collected this summer into so many bytes of electronic memory. Putting the facts onto the screen was so much more neat, more satisfying, than gathering them on the nunatak. But his first surprise upon meeting William was that this man no longer liked to discuss computers—that, in fact, he no longer owned one. So they had found little to talk about, and Ronald had formed without knowing it a certain basic distrust of the man.

So even if William had not been walking a hundred feet behind him at the end of the rope, hidden by a curtain of fog, Ronald would not have disclosed his mind. He heard only the occasional chink of the spike of William's ax on the ice and felt hardly a tug on the rope. William knew how to walk on a glacier without pulling his partner about, in spite of Ronald's stopping and starting to search the way. But there, ahead, was the first wand, a green bamboo garden stake with a small orange flag tied round the top. His crampons settled into snow. The way would be easier now. He could see their morning's tracks in the firn, and where he couldn't, it was only a matter of charting his course from wand to wand.

Given the chance, he might have talked with William about the vectors of glacier mechanics, about the logistics of planning a survey, about the way in which a theodolite works. Something that would not have occurred to Ronald to share was the state of his feelings for Jennifer, though she too was much on his mind. Was it possible to be so annoyed with someone you were in love with—engaged to even? The thought itself was a deep annoyance, since it violated the defined commitment he thought he had made.

He knew he was what his old friends called a science geek, someone who never went anywhere, not even to a party, without his pocket calculator. Not that he went to many parties of any sort, wild or tame, for he did not drink and was much too inhibited to dance. (He was, after all, the son of a preacher. His father had died in the pulpit he pounded, excoriating the children of Israel who played about the golden calf.) From the day he had met her, Jennifer had touched his soul with a needed warmth and spontaneity which though he had not been able to share he could at least appreciate. Jennifer loved to perform herself for him and did not seem to expect him to be more than a grateful audience. That is, until recently.

As their summer in the mountains had passed, he had sensed her growing impatience with his native passivity. She expressed it in barbs and in outright objections to his dedication to research. Could he help it that Dr. Howe was his major professor? Was it his fault he aspired to become a junior version of her father? The closer he grew to the tutelage of

Professor Howe, the farther she removed her affection. By the end of the summer he had figured this out in the form of an equation: as *a* approaches *b* . . .

It presented him with yet another personal dilemma, no less ethical perhaps than the choice of whether to blow the whistle on the possibility of a *jokulhlaup*. Of course, there was a way of joining the two. He could relieve his conscience with a note to Escee, alienate Dr. Howe forever, and thus win the undying love of his fiancée who by definition should already be in love with him anyway—whatever *love* was. And if it were an anonymous note, Dr. Howe would never know, though Jennifer could, and—

His thoughts were cut short by a sudden unsettling of snow at his feet. His stomach made a quiet lurch, as one's stomach does when an elevator begins its plunge. And before he could even think to call out, Ronald found himself dangling at the end of the rope in a blue-lit cavern. Over his head spun a bright round hole in an arched roof of rotten firn. His hand still grasped the head of his ax, which hung comically useless above an abyss where the blue walls dropped into darkness.

And comical is the way he felt—not so much frightened as desperately foolish. In his mind he heard Jennifer laughing derisively. *Watch your step, Mr. Science!* He reached his ax in front of him. With the tip of the spike at the end of the shaft he could just touch the closest wall. There was no question of climbing out with crampons and ax. He would have to prussik up the rope.

Blocks of snow came cascading onto his shoulders. "You O.K., Ronald?" William's face was peering down from the now enlarged hole above.

"Fine," said Ronald. "Just hanging around."

William laughed, not in mockery, but in a way that put Ronald at ease. Suddenly there was something he liked about this man.

"The rope's fixed," William called down. "I've got it anchored on a fluke. Have enough prussiks?"

"Plenty," said Ronald, fingering the loops at his waist.

"I'll back off then," William said, "before I join you."

Ronald had never actually fallen into a crevasse before, but he had practiced getting in and out of them many times. One way of gauging the health and history of a glacier was to rappel into an open crevasse alongside a measuring tape and to note the depth of each layer of accumulation of snow turned ice. Each year's layer was separated from the next by a thin brown line, dirt blown up on the old summer surface. It was a little like counting tree rings—or more like bathtub rings. The farther down you went, the closer the rings drew together. Here the firn had compacted itself by its own weight into blue and then into black ice,

> snow on snow
> Snow on snow,
> In the bleak mid-winter
> Long ago.

As Ronald clipped his ax to his harness with a carabiner, he measured the strata on the wall before him with a newly trained eye. The top layer ended just over his head—this year's addition—and the firn below it was a tinge grayer. He counted six bands down into dimness. There were the snows of yesteryear—a practical answer to an elegiac question.

To business. He wrapped a cord in a sliding prussik knot on the rope, attached a green nylon sling and secured it around the instep of his left boot, careful not to puncture the sling with the fangs of his crampon. Then he tied another prussik above the first and clipped this second cord to the harness at his waist.

"Climbing!" he called to the empty hole. He stood up on his

sling-wrapped foot and watched the prussik tighten on the rope. Then he slid the higher knot up, sat down on it with his full weight, and raised his slung foot once again. By this tedious process, inches at a time, he swung and twirled his way up the rope.

His progress slowed at the very top where the rope lay partially buried in the lip. This hidden crevasse was capped by a roof some three feet thick, and when Ronald had fallen through, the rope had cut into the edge of the hole. He tried to shove his prussiks ahead, but they would not follow the rope through the snow.

"Stuck?" said William. He was just out of sight up over the lip. "Excavate a little. I've got the shaft of my ax beneath the rope back here. It won't saw in any farther."

Ronald gingerly unclipped his ax and pawed at the snow above with the adze. Chunks and clods came streaming down against his chest, some falling inside his parka and lodging next to his tender skin.

"Just one thing," said William casually. "Try not to cut the rope."

Ronald imagined the consequences, and took care. A few more minutes of chilling work cleared the way. He edged his prussiks up the trough that he had made until they neared the ax at the surface. Then William reached it down to pull him out the rest of the way. Ronald was glad that William's ice ax was so long. Grasping the head of that dark smooth shaft was like grasping a hand sent down into deep waters.

They sat together back from the hole. Ronald was panting, his body shivering without his permission. He felt wet all over, from sweat or melting snow or both. William put his arm around him, and that was good. Then there was warm lemonade in a bottle, and chocolate to eat, and the world was a better place. The fog all about them was kind comfort, a welcome back to the land of the living.

"You don't find many roofed-up cracks like that in September," William marveled. "Count yourself a discoverer."

Ronald smiled. The fog lifted a tiny bit, and he saw the silhouette of a ribbon-capped wand far off to the right. In his musings he had swerved off route.

"Getting late in the afternoon," William said. "I suppose we could get the data book another day?"

Ronald stiffened. "Oh, no. We're close. I'm alright—really." He stood up and began to untie his prussiks.

William looked at him dubiously, but Ronald insisted.

"Let me go first on the rope at least—the last thing you need is another plunge."

"But I know the way," Ronald said—"at least, when I'm paying attention I do. It gets a bit tricky ahead at the schrund." Ronald wondered if William admired his pluck or scorned his foolishness. In reality it was only fear—if he failed to recover his data, he might as well hop into the bergschrund *sans* rope as face Dr. Howe again.

In the end William merely made sure that Ronald had emptied the snow from his clothes, and let him continue. Ronald regained the misplaced wand, and watching closely, found the next, and the next, and the next after that in the darkening clouds. They would need to move quickly on the descent to avoid the coming of rain and night.

When he reached the schrund with its sagging bridge, Ronald brought William up beside him and asked for a belay. William nodded, and sank the shaft of his ax in the firn until only the head was poking out. Then he knelt and braced the head with his boot, wrapping the rope around leather and shaft in an S-curve. Ronald worried a bit about the strength of the wood, but said nothing.

"Belay's on," William said, and worked the rope around boot and ax while Ronald edged his way down the bridge. He experimentally plunged his ax in front of him at arm's length, doubting the firmness of the causeway more than he ever had before. At the lowest point he looked into the chasm on his left. The upper wall, banded white, then gray, then blue, then black, was much higher than the one behind him, and more than slightly overhung. The noise of meltwater rushed to his ears from somewhere very far below. It continued, he knew, to where the schrund pinched together some hundred yards off in impassable chaos. There the meltwater doubtless entered a cave in the ice, perhaps one that Dr. Howe and the others had already mapped with Brunton compass.

Ronald turned to the ladder of kicked footsteps that surmounted the upper wall ahead and slotted his boots, one at a time, in each pocket with great care. If any part of the bridge broke he thought it would be this upper ramp, ready to slough when gravity beckoned. But he reached the top without incident and called to William that by the time he had run out the rope he would have William on belay. There was no need for William to belay him any longer.

A few more steps brought Ronald to the projection of rock at the trashy foot of the nunatak. He stopped for a moment at the margin of the snow and peered upward into the fog. It was eerily quiet in an anticlimactic sort of way. He saw nothing, really, certainly not the top of the nunatak, but then a gust of wind rearranged the fog and he saw something indeed.

Halfway up the rock slope, the obese marmot sat on a ledge with a yellow notebook in its paws. Its teeth were tearing slowly at the pages, and its cheeks were just beginning to bulge with masticated theodolite readings. The marmot looked at Ronald impassively with dead black eyes.

"Drop it!" screamed Ronald. Without thinking, he lunged up the slope, clashing at the rocks with his crampons. Strangely, the marmot went on chewing and did not move.

"Give me the book!" Ronald shouted. He was almost up to the marmot now, and leapt forward with arms outstretched as if to seize it by the throat. His hands were just about to close on the book—or on what was left of it, anyhow—when Ronald felt a sharp jerk from behind on the rope which sent him reeling back down the slope. His crampons caught on one another, and he somersaulted down the scree and landed with a jolt against the pillar of rock by the snow.

For a few moments he lay there in a crumpled tangle, cursing his fall and the unlucky loss of his data. Then he realized what had happened. In his rush to reclaim his book from the marmot, he had pulled William into the schrund, where now, no doubt, he was dangling like a marionette, wondering why Ronald had popped his strings. "You idiot!" he muttered to himself.

Much more slowly than he would have liked to, he rose to his feet, bracing himself against the steady pull of the rope, and slipped a sling around the pillar. He tied a prussik around the rope and clipped it off to the sling with a carabiner. Then, hands shaking, he untied the slack from his waist and knotted it to the sling with a bowline for good measure. The rope was anchored.

He glanced upward and saw neither book nor marmot. Below him the taut rope disappeared into graying snow and fog. He did not yell, knowing that William would not be able to hear his voice until he got to the very edge. He tied on his other prussik, clipped it to his harness, and headed toward the brink, sliding the knot down the rope as he went.

He had not gone far before he saw the marmot again. It was bent over astride the rope just above the lip of the schrund. The book was gone.

Ronald stumbled closer. "Beat it!" he shouted. "I'm warning you!" He waved his ice ax menacingly. When he was almost upon the marmot again he saw exactly what it was doing, and stopped for a moment in sheer despair. Quite deliberately, the creature was gnawing at the sheath of the rope, worrying away at the woven strands like a dog at a bone.

In a fury Ronald leapt forward and swung his ice ax hard through the air, aiming for the creature's neck with the sharp-edged adze. At the last instant the marmot shot aside. And the adze sliced neatly through the rope, finishing what teeth had begun. As Ronald fell against the pull of his prussik he watched the rope fly over the edge and flicker in the fog like the tongue of a snake. He lay facedown in the cold-churned snow. On his neck he felt the beating of rain.

5

JENNIFER FOUND HERSELF STANDING on rough-hewn planks, and wondered where the heather had gone. The ax in her hands was slowly dripping blood on the floor. She was in the center of a fair-sized room amid stone walls and wooden rafters. A generous fireplace stood at one end. Water was streaming down two small windows, and an open door let in the sound of falling rain. She remained as rooted as the ax had been, too frightened to move a single step.

After listening to the rainy silence a long time, Jennifer looked down at the ax and saw that the blood was no longer welling out from the shaft. The rose lay crushed on the floor at her feet. She stooped and took it in her blood-soaked hands. It was the first she had moved.

Emboldened, she stepped to the open door. The rose was real, the floor was real—and so was the rain as she stood in the doorway. The fog had lifted, and in the light of late afternoon she looked down the same gentle slopes of dark green heather and rusty grass to the slate waters of Chambers Lake. There was nothing for it but to traipse back to camp and consult with Gwen on these odd things.

She was three steps out the door when she took in the shore of the lake. She stopped, stunned. Where the ungainly clutter of tents had been, summer headquarters of Dr. Howe's prestigious Glacier and Nature Project, the GNP, lay only an empty space of heather. The camp was gone.

Walking towards her, however, from the vacant site were two tall figures, a man and a woman by their gait. Jennifer hoped the woman was Gwen; she could not guess who the man might be. But she also feared it was not Gwen, since so much else was not as it should be. Suddenly the strange cabin felt more inviting.

She retreated to the shelter of the open doorway and even glanced about the room for a place to hide. There was a bed, a stool, a rocking chair, and in one corner a small table. A black iron kettle hung in the fireplace, and for a moment she thought of curling up inside it. But without quite choosing to do so, she stayed in the door and gave herself up to meeting whoever was coming this way. For a moment she wondered how Goldilocks felt, but then recalled that Goldilocks had had the good fortune to be asleep when the Three Bears returned home. She put the rose on the doorstep and tried to wipe her hands clean on the wet heather, thinking she would not make such a good impression with blood-soaked paws. But her hands remained red, as if stained with dye.

As the figures approached, Jennifer saw that each was hooded with a brown cloak, their faces so cowled against the rain that she could not see them. They did not appear to have noticed her; by the pointing and nodding of the hoods at each other, the pair appeared deep in conversation. But when within just a few steps of the cabin, the larger of the two pulled back his hood and looked straight at Jennifer.

"Well, there you are. Caught red-handed." Then he laughed in a rough but merry sort of way. He had a smooth bald head with a ruff of white hair about his ears and a large plain face, set off by a ruddy nose.

"For shame, Sir Chambers. 'Tis not a matter for lightness," said the other. This was the woman. She too put back the hood of her cloak and advanced with grave but gentle eyes. What struck Jennifer immediately was that the eyes were green, like

Gwen's. But the woman's hair was a deep rich brown, not blonde and braided. It was someone else entirely.

"Oh, child, child," the woman sighed, and grasped both of her bloodstained hands. Jennifer felt ashamed and comforted all at once.

Then the woman stooped down and took up the mangled rose on the step. She looked at it sorrowfully, and Jennifer wished with all her heart she were back in the cook tent stirring a pot of dried peas, bulgur, and tuna. From within her cloak the woman took a small glass vial and folded Jennifer's hands around it. Without a word she held the flower over the vial and began to squeeze—hard, the way one squeezes a sponge dry.

The man stepped up and watched closely.

A sweet clear liquid, not at all the color of blood, began to drip into the vial. When the vial was full, the woman opened her hands and they were empty. The rose was gone. She capped the vial with a crystal stopper, and Jennifer offered it back to her.

"It is for you to take," the woman said, "to help the wounded sleep. When it is time to use it, you will know. Keep it till then."

Jennifer nodded timidly. "Can you tell me," she asked, "who you are, and where I am?"

"Why, yes," the man put in. "All this hocus-pocus and no proper welcome. Let's go inside out of this rain and introduce ourselves, of course." He ushered them into the darkened cabin in much the same way that Jennifer's father had brought Escee through the door of the mess tent the night before—with the same harmless, officious grandeur.

Then he took Jennifer's hand and made a small bow. "Sir Chambers," he said, "at your service. You are, at present, a guest in my cabin, on the shores of my lake. Mine in a manner of speaking, of course—can't say that they're mine in any but the loosest proprietary fashion. They might as well be yours, or hers, and in fact they are, and yet none of ours at all. That's what I call a conundrum of ownership. And who, may I please ask, are you?"

I wish I knew, Jennifer thought.

Before she could say, Chambers continued, "Friend or foe, we'll show you kindness, no worry for that. A fire is just what's needed now, and a pot of soup. What say you to lentil soup—or perhaps it's dried peas you like?"

"Shush," said the woman. "You know we have no time for that. Let the girl speak, and we'll be on our way."

"I—I'm Jennifer Howe," said Jennifer. "I'm not sure how—"

"Is it Jennifer Howe or I'm-Not-Sure Howe?" interrupted Sir Chambers. "I'm not sure which, though I'm sure you aren't—a witch, that is." He laughed again, the same rough-merry way. "But then again, *numquam certus*—I'm never sure, just like you. We've established something in common, you see—perhaps the basis for a lasting friendship."

The woman put her hand on his arm and looked at him severely. "Go on, child," she said to Jennifer. "You must bear with us."

Jennifer looked at each of them in turn, feeling more confused than ever. "What I mean—I think—is that I'm not sure how I got here. In this cabin, that is. And I'm sorry about the rose and the ax—they weren't mine to disturb at all. If you'd just take me back to my friends who are camped nearby—at least they were—except I don't know—and—" And here Jennifer did a very unscientific thing—she began to cry.

The woman gathered her in her arms. "What's done is done, Jennifer. And all that is done you do not yet know. It cannot be helped, but it has been helped. We're here to give you—Sir Chambers and I—some of the help that is already given."

These words struck Jennifer so strangely that she began to stop crying out of sheer curiosity.

"My name is Lady Demaris. Perhaps you have been to my cottage before?"

"*Your* cottage?" Jennifer exclaimed.

"In trust, you understand," Chambers interjected, "as I was explaining."

"But that's where Gwen and William live."

"Precisely who we're concerned about now," said Lady Demaris. "From what Chambers has just seen in his lake, your friend William is in sore need."

"But he's up on the glacier, not in the lake."

"Exactly," said Chambers. "I saw him where he wasn't. And if we don't manage to get to him soon, he won't be at all. So excuse me while I pack a few things for our walk up the hill." With that he lit a couple of candles and began to rummage through a chest and to take down things from a shelf over the fireplace.

Jennifer listened to the rain on the roof. She felt rather dismal about the prospect of hiking back up to the glacier with this odd man in the wet gloom. "What about Ronald?" she plaintively asked.

"The boy with him?" said Lady Demaris. "It sounds as if that has been your question for a long time. Perhaps you are the one who can answer it."

Jennifer blushed and thought of nothing to say. She was glad when Chambers was standing with them once again, tin lantern in hand and a canvas rucksack heaped on his back. Jennifer put on her cagoule and wool balaclava without being asked and tucked the vial in a deep front pocket. She picked up the bloodstained ax again, then quickly offered to put it down.

"For now it is yours," said Lady Demaris. "It was once my

sister's, and still is, most so when in other hands. What you have won by violence, take."

Grotesque as the wounded ice ax was, Jennifer was glad to keep it. There is something good about having the head of an ax in your hand when heading into the cold and dark. With the coming of the rain it was nearly evening.

"You are staying?" said Chambers to Lady Demaris.

"This time, yes. I have a journey shortly to go which must begin tonight. Take young Jennifer to the cave. I am bound otherwhere."

"Farewell then," said Chambers rather stiffly. He seemed to be hiding some disappointment. "Until the Feast of Free Waters, perhaps."

"Perhaps," echoed Lady Demaris. Then she took Jennifer in her arms again. "Take courage," she said. "We will see what good may be worked out of evil. Often more than we desire, let alone deserve—any of us. You have only done what we ask or think. I shall see you again, and then perhaps all shall be well—all manner of thing shall be well."

She kissed Jennifer on the forehead, and Jennifer backed into Chambers on the step while mumbling good-bye. Chambers steered her out the door, and they were gone.

Though dusky and damp it was not quite dark, and the light from the lantern which Chambers held was still superfluous. He led Jennifer at a quick pace on a small path that contoured gently up the hill. When it dipped to meet the stream from the glacier she recognized the grassy bank on which she and Gwen had rested and talked on the way down. *Poor Gwen*, she thought—*quite disappeared. And William hurt?* She thought of the snowbridge over the bergschrund and wondered if it had finally collapsed. And if it had, how would Sir Chambers have known about it? She wanted to ask him more concerning what he had seen, but the stream was so loud, and the rain was beating so hard all around them, and they were both so wrapped in cloak and cagoule, that she would have to be at his shoulder to talk. And the path was so narrow, and the footing so dim, that she had to walk in file behind him.

So she trudged uphill in silence, grateful not to be carrying a pack, but feeling the rain pelt cold and hard on her back and shoulders, and wishing she had sealed the seams of her cagoule more recently, for the water was gradually seeping through. Her boots, too, already damp from a day of use, were saturating her socks to the skin. In the last few weeks, since the softer snow had melted down to firn and ice, she had neglected to waterproof the leather.

By the time they reached the end of the heather and began to stumble through the moraines, the lantern had become of use. The light that shone through the holes in the tin was just enough to speckle the path for each step. It was truly dark. Jennifer stayed on Chambers' heels, not conscious of anything now except where to place her next foot. So it came as a surprise when Chambers stopped, and the rain with him. She was not so silly as to run into the back of him, but in catching herself she suddenly slipped, and found herself thrust on a wall of ice. It was strangely quiet except for the hollow splash of the stream which sounded in echoes.

"A fine and private place," said Chambers, "and a dry one too. Watch your step, and welcome to Chambers' Chambers, as I call them. Not that they're mine, you understand."

"I've been here before," Jennifer told him, irritated by his condescension. "At least right here, at the entrance. My father is mapping these caves, you realize. He knows all about them."

"Does he, now?" Chambers said, pulling back the hood of his cloak and wrinkling up his massive brow. "What an admirable thing, to know all about them, as you say. I could never claim so much. My aim is merely to know them, and to know myself. Probably the same aspiration. So far, except in perhaps the tiniest moments, I have failed."

Jennifer looked at him curiously.

"But that doesn't mean I can't guide you to the living heart, the center of search, the crystal chamber. I know how to get there, just like your father probably does. The problem is, I never know what to do—or how to be—once I get there. I'd love to have his confidence—pack in a ruler, calculate the cubic cubits, and walk away knowing all about it. But I have an idea the beauty of the place, the essence of it, grows out of some immeasurable goodness, and after that, some immeasurable tragedy, and beyond that, I'd like to know."

He was not being comical now. Jennifer could see the earnest sense of quest in his eyes as he looked down the cave and into the shadows beyond the lamplight. Sir Chambers seemed a pathetically unlikely candidate for ever finding the goddess within. For a moment she wished he could cross the barrier of gender and so have at least some hope.

"But it's time we were going. There's tragedy enough at hand if my intuition serves me right. You don't have anything for your feet, do you—to keep you up on the ice ahead?"

"No, I'm afraid I gave my crampons away this afternoon."

Chambers took his pack off and fished out two pair of black iron spikes that he called *creepers.* "Strap these on," he said.

As Jennifer did so she noticed that her hands, streaming wet from their hike in the rain, were still blood red. She wiped them together with no result. Her ice ax, equally washed by the rain, was no cleaner. She stood up to follow Chambers into the cave and tried not to think about it, but of course she did. An unwelcome echo came to her mind:

> *Therein the patient*
> *Must minister to himself.*

She felt the impossibility of cure.

The cave at the entrance where they stood was ten feet

across and not quite as high. It was floored with rubble, and the walls and ceiling were smoothly scalloped out of clear black ice that shone like obsidian in the light. Jennifer could see starred explosions beneath the surface, the flaws and stresses of a hidden world. They followed the stream up over the stones until it too was flowing on ice, more quietly now, slipping in a sinuous runnel. More than once, Jennifer nearly stepped in the water because she thought it was part of the floor.

Before very long the passage narrowed, then climbed steeply, arcing left. The stream at their side found voice again, the continuous rush of a clear cascade. She found it soothing to pick her way up the ice beside it, sometimes setting the teeth of her ax to steady her balance on the ascent. But after a while her calves ached, and she longed for rest.

Just when her legs were beginning to tremble beyond her control, the passage opened into a level chamber, its invisible ceiling supported by pillars of silvered ice. Three separate tunnels, each bringing a small stream, led up and away. But for now they paused.

Chambers held up his lantern alongside the closest pillar, and Jennifer thought she glimpsed a ceiling some thirty feet up. "Moulins," he said. "Water falling from chutes overhead. Up higher they won't be frozen."

The walls of the room were a creamy mixture of blue and white, sometimes mingled in brilliant turquoise. The waterfall pillars were solid, brilliant, statuesque. Jennifer felt as if she had entered an airy, tasteful gallery of sculpture in a museum. She heard herself saying, "It is lovely indeed, it is lovely indeed."

Chambers bobbed his head and smiled, as if to hint there was better to come.

He chose the center of the three passages. It wound less steeply than before, back and forth, serpentine fashion, further up and further in. By and by Jennifer heard the crashing of water up ahead, and around a corner, falling to the floor like great shafts of liquid light, were three live moulins, raging and hissing from ceiling to floor. They slalomed around them, hooding their faces against the spray, and continued on past more pillars, frozen again. The ice was white on the ceiling and upper walls, with a wainscoting of pure black. Once more, the passage was narrowing.

Soon they had to walk in the stream single file, turning and slipping between the walls in the smallest places. The water was only ankle deep, but Jennifer's feet became very cold, and she began to wonder if it were possible, and how it would feel, to fall through a moulin underfoot. And when she slithered against the walls she felt they were moving in on her, traveling their daily foot in a moment to catch her by surprise.

She was about to insist they turn around when Chambers gained a steep dry passage that left the stream. The walls opened out a bit, and after a few twists and turns, Chambers came to a sudden halt. This time Jennifer did bump into the back of him, and not so much the back of him as into the arm that held the lantern, which crashed to the floor and extinguished itself.

But it did not matter. The chamber in which they found themselves was already illuminated with four tall candles in candlesticks. The walls and ceiling were coated with crystals that reflected the light like the hung glass of fine and feathery chandeliers. In this light she saw much in an instant.

Amidst the candles, bandaged and bleeding and lying on a bed of blankets, was the body of William—or what Jennifer hoped was still William himself. At his side knelt an aged man in a cloak like Chambers', the hood pulled back to make room for a long white mane and beard. And next to this man, soaked and pale and staring at Jennifer, stood a mournful version of Ronald Miller. He held a bloody ax in his hands. To the wrist they were coated a brilliant red.

6

"GREETINGS, BROTHER," Chambers said to the white-haired man. "Welcome." He spoke as if it were the other who had just arrived and Chambers who had been there first—which, in his loosely proprietary way, he probably had.

Ignoring Ronald, he approached the prostrate body of William and solemnly asked, "Is the hurt unto death?"

Jennifer sidled up to Ronald and grasped his hand. She felt it shivering in her own, and looked down to see their fingers interlaced in blood. The same blood? She thought about the odd possibility.

"Unto death?" repeated the man. He was tall and sad—his face a crag and his eyes deep-set. There was something noble but used up about him. "It is not given for us to know, but it well may be."

William was breathing raggedly now. He tossed his head from side to side and let out a low moan like a wind far down in the cavern. His temples and forehead were bandaged with a swath of cloth. If the deep bright stain on the cloth told true, they were bleeding still. His side also was terribly wounded. There where William's parka was torn, the sad old man held a thick compress to staunch the welling.

"And you, my daughter," the old man said, fixing his gaze upon Jennifer, "what do you bring in your bloodstained hands?"

Jennifer let go of Ronald and looked at her hands in blank

confusion. She brought guilt, perhaps. And she supposed she brought the goddess within. But neither seemed to be of much help in the present moment.

"The vial," said Chambers, pointing to the pouch of her cagoule.

Jennifer had forgotten. She found the vial and held it out. "I do bring something," she timidly said. "A gift, I think. It is every drop of a red, red rose that I broke from this ax and that Lady Demaris crushed in her hand. She said it would make the wounded sleep. It is all I have, and it's not mine. I stole it, but she made it good."

Jennifer still held out the vial, but the old man did not reach for it. "The same hands that broke the rose must bring it to his lips," he said. "Step up, daughter, and do not be afraid. You bring help, not harm, now."

Jennifer left Ronald's side and edged behind the aged man to William's upturned face. They made a symmetrical company then, she at his head, the two white-bearded ones facing each other on either side, and Ronald standing at William's feet. Between each of them, at the corners of the body, the tall candles burned quietly. The chamber glowed like a holy place, and when Jennifer lifted William's head and put the vial to his lips she felt as if she were following the written rites to a ceremony. She was not taking action but performing a role. It was the difference between breaking a rose and being broken by it.

The distillation, sweet and clear, slipped between the swollen lips like a sigh recalled, if there be such a thing, and immediately William lay still and calm, quietly breathing. The old man lifted his hands from the compress and examined the gash in William's side.

"He bleeds no more," the man announced, and all four of them, just like William, visibly relaxed.

"Doesn't she have the touch, though," Chambers said admiringly. And by the way that he said it, turning his head and nodding toward the passage behind him, it was obvious he was not referring to Jennifer. "One fine woman, I always say. One fine woman. Be a lucky man to—"

The other man, looking not at all lucky but still quite lorn, interrupted Chambers as if he had not been speaking at all. "And now," he said, turning to Ronald and then back to Jennifer, "it is time to wash your hands and your axes. Go both of you down the eastern passage till you come to the river, and cleanse yourselves. Then I shall tell you what you shall do."

Jennifer and Ronald each nodded submissively. Jennifer started for the passage at William's feet by which she had come; Ronald, his eyes self-consciously downcast, turned to an exit at William's head.

The old man stopped them. "No—together. The *eastern* passage." He pointed to a tunnel behind him that led away from William's side.

"Oh," they both said. Chambers offered his lantern to Ronald, who accepted it with mumbled thanks and relit the wick inside on one of the candles burning between them. Holding the lantern at arm's length as if it were a bucket of shame, he shuffled down the correct corridor with Jennifer at his heels. The way gently descended through clear black walls that gradually opened till Jennifer could comfortably walk at Ronald's side. It was a relief somehow to escape the chamber.

"Who's the old guy?" Jennifer asked. "And what in Mary Shelley's name are we doing here?"

"Just what I was going to ask you, Jen," Ronald replied in a shivering voice, "though at the moment, God's name is enough for me. Who's the fellow you showed up with?"

"I asked first. And tell me, will you, what happened to William? Somehow I feel I had something to do with it. If only I hadn't forgotten the data book. Though that's the least of it, I suppose."

She saw that he was averting his eyes. "Ronald?" She

paused. "Did you—were you . . ." She trailed off, not knowing how to put into words the symmetry of guilt that she guessed. By his silence she knew they shared one fault. In the spotty light she slipped her arm about his side and groaned to herself as she felt him quiver.

After a long quiet, peppered by the tapping of their axes on the ice, Ronald said, "Well, it's Garth. That's what he says his name is. And good thing I ran into him too. Otherwise I'd be—listen! Do you hear water, Jen?"

They stopped, and she nodded in affirmation. Round one more bend they came upon the glistening bank of a deep dark stream that crossed their passage from right to left. It was just wider than they could jump—and fortunately they did not care to. Ronald set the lantern between them and knelt on the ice, laying his ax carefully aside. Jennifer knelt and laid her ax aside as well.

They looked at each other for an awkward moment, then plunged in their hands and kept them there, scrubbing them desperately one against the other. Cold pierced flesh like little knives. Jennifer gasped at the steely pain, and tears formed in her eyes and fell. She could of course have removed her hands at any moment, but could not bear the thought of seeing them even partially red again.

In time she was sure that her hands were no longer freezing but burning, as they did when she put them in boiled dishwater before it cooled in the entrance of the cook tent. The fire and ice of the world were upon her. After much longer than she thought she could stand it, she raised her arms, and so did Ronald. She looked at her throbbing hands in the lamplight and found them clean, white as the crystals in the chamber behind them. Her tears redoubled, and she saw that Ronald was weeping too, something she had not known him to do. There was no blood left on his hands either. They stiffly intertwined their fingers above the lantern, hardly able to feel the comfort of cold flesh, and waited for warmth and strength to return.

"Now," said Ronald, still sniffling a little, "if you can face the prospect of doing it again, we've got to wash the axes too." He always liked a complete task.

Jennifer shuddered. She'd had enough purging for one day—perhaps enough for a lifetime. On the other hand (though she still wasn't sure she could feel one apart from the other), she couldn't see trudging back up to the chamber with scrubbed palms and bloody axes. It would be like cleaning her father's fish and returning his pocketknife smeared and fouled.

"Alright," she said. It was only then, as she grasped her ax and held it out with two hands, as if in offering, that she noticed that the ax Ronald held over the water beside her was not his own. "Whose is that?" she asked. "It's too long to be yours. Is it William's?"

Ronald nodded and lowered it carefully into the water. "I'll explain," he said. "I had to leave mine on top—for an anchor." But instead of explaining further he moaned with the force of cold renewed in his fingers, and so did Jennifer, who had settled her ax in the stream as well.

She squeezed her hands back and forth along the shaft and took special care, and quite literally special pains, to wipe the blood from the pick and the adze on the silvery head. The metal ached even more than the wood, and once again the suffering became unbearable. But as she lost the sense of touch from her hands, half afraid she would lose her hold on the ax in her numbness, she felt something quite odd occurring. The spike of the shaft seemed suddenly blunt. The shaft itself became thick and round, and its upper end, as she traveled its shape, was growing wide and thin somehow, until there was—well, it was quite impossible—until there was no head at all. Jennifer lifted her ax from the water, and Ronald did the same. She held in her hands, and he held in his, a dripping wooden oar.

Their surprise was so great they forgot the pain of cold in their fingers. Quietly they stood their oars blade up on the ice and knocked them together—the tips were even. William's ax had been longer than the one Jennifer had taken, but the only difference between the oars was the color of wood—both clean of blood, but one, William's, dark and smoky like oiled oak, and the other, from the sister of Lady Demaris, clean and white like fresh-split ash. They rose astonished, unable to put words to wonder, and held their dripping oars before them as minutes before they had held their axes. A few drops kissed the lid of the lantern and extinguished themselves in a tiny hiss. The black walls danced in the light, and the deep dark stream flowed quietly on.

Jennifer was on the point of stating the obvious weirdness of what had just happened, and was in fact ransacking her mind for some metamorphic precedent in Ovid. (She had read him on the recommendation of one of the passionate health store poets, with particular attention to Diana the huntress and the happy demise of Actaeon.) But before she could speak, something large came bumping down the stream from the darkness. Ronald encircled her shoulders protectively (something Diana would never have stood for) and held out his oar in a defensive posture, wishing it were still an ax.

The thing came looming into the light—not an animate foe at all, but a large wooden boat, square at the stern, arching high to a pointed prow, and almost as wide as the channel itself. Its wooden benches were perfectly empty. As the boat came alongside them they each leaned out and laid hold of the gunwale. For a moment the current tugged the boat against their grip. Then in tacit agreement they slid it sideways onto shore. The keel caught on the lip of the bank, but when they dropped their oars and put all four of their hands to the task, the boat soon listed full on the ice beside the lantern.

They panted a little, hands on hips, and wondered even more. "Hey," said Jennifer, trying to sound flippant, "cruise ships and candlelight. What more could we ask? Seems to me our little adventure is taking a rather romantic turn." She embraced him dramatically and murmured, "Sail with me to the Nile, dahlink."

Ronald was singularly unresponsive. "No," he said, "let's get back to the others."

Jennifer shrugged and picked up the lantern. They had no sooner turned up the passage, however, than they saw Chambers descending towards them holding out a second lantern he must have taken from his pack. Behind him came Garth with a measured tread, carefully bearing William in his arms. Jennifer had had no idea the old man was so strong.

When Chambers reached them he held his lantern over the boat and whistled softly. "Why, Amoenas," he said, as if addressing a stray cow, "what are you doing busting loose from your moorings like that? Never could keep you in just one place."

"She has only spared you the trouble," said Garth. He approached the boat and carefully laid his burden in it upon the blanket which had swaddled the body in his arms. William's head he neatly pillowed in the prow, and tucked his feet just beneath the rowing bench. The boat was still listing, and Ronald and Jennifer carefully rocked it upright to afford a more decent resting place. They stood on either side of the prow, looking down at William's face. He was still and peaceful, breathing quietly. Chambers unfolded another wool blanket from out of his pack and spread it over the sleeping form, tucking it under the motionless chin in a motherly way that surprised Jennifer very much.

Then Garth, standing grim at the stern of the boat, spoke

again. "I send you on a journey, my children, for your cleansing and for his healing. I know that now your hands are clean, and the axes are washed, but these things are but a beginning. From here the stream leads through the dark to the eastern highlands, and thence south and west to Amoenas Gorge, where you will find rest at the Tower of Otium. From Otium it is still many miles to the Western Sea, and there your charge will be at an end. At the shore you will meet those to whom you may give the body at rest, and they will accomplish the final healing in the course, perhaps, of many years.

"I say all that I know, all that has been given to me, and leave you now with benediction:

> *"The tongues of ice and water go with thee,*
> *The arms of the floating maiden support thee,*
> *The song of the ouzel lead thee aright,*
> *And may thy voice find praise with these.*

"Farewell," he said. "Seek thy rest on the restless river."

Chambers tossed his pack into the boat and fixed their lantern to a tiny post at the back of the stern. At his nod they helped him skid the boat back into the stream, and he held it there while Ronald and Jennifer took off their crampons and clambered in, Jennifer thinking that this could be the stupidest thing she had ever done. She took her seat on a bench by the lantern, facing Ronald, who sat amidships on the rowing bench. His feet straddled the upturned toes of William's boots that poked out from underneath. Chambers was handing him both oars and showing him how to fit them through the oarlocks to row.

"But you won't need them here, where the channel is narrow. Keep them inside the boat just now so they don't get broken. Follow your nose—or William's perhaps—and let Jennifer do your seeing for you. There are plenty more candles in the pack, and blankets too, and a bit to eat if you get hungry. You should reach the snout by morning light, or evening at the very latest. It's a long ways, but the dark and the ice do not last forever. All glaciers have an end, and all rivers their first beginning. The Alpha really is the Omega, when you think about it, though for a while you'll be traveling in between."

Jennifer wanted to ask about this, but already he had pushed them away.

"*Semper lentus!*" Chambers called after them. "*Festina lente!* Don't go too fast if you can help it, and hasten slowly. Those oars may have a bit of magic, but I know for a fact the boat does not. On ice or rock it will stave in and sink before you can say—"

What Chambers could and might have said was lost in an indistinct series of echoes, for the boat had bumped around a turn and cut him away from sight and sound. For just a moment Jennifer saw the glow of his lamp from around the bend, and then they were floating quite alone down a keyhole passage filled with water. She reached her hands to the walls and ceiling and felt them glide beneath her fingers, cold and hard.

7

"So THEN WHAT HAPPENED?" Jennifer said in an awful whisper. She had already told Ronald her story—about the rose and the cabin and Lady Demaris—and now was hearing his. It was a good time for telling stories, for although they were still in the boat with William beneath the glacier, they were no longer coursing a narrow passage but plowing about on a huge black lake in a large cavern, so tall they could not spy the ceiling. Ronald was rowing as Chambers had shown him, but somewhat haphazardly since there was no real current to follow. He was just beginning to think, in fact, that he might be better off not rowing at all, for if the lake had an outlet, as it no doubt did, the boat would soonest find it by drifting. But just sitting there, oars dripping into unfathomable darkness, felt so forlorn to both of them that he kept rowing to prove to himself that they did exist.

"What happened," said Ronald, "was that I was so stunned after cutting the rope that I lay in the snow, in shock I suppose, till the rain revived me. It had started to rain."

"Just then?"

"Just then."

"Oh, Ronald," she moaned. "That's when it started for me too—when the ax bled, and I pulled it out. Don't you see? It was I who really severed the rope—when I severed the rose."

Ronald stopped rowing and touched her shoulders with both wet oars. "Fallacy, Jen: *post hoc ergo propter hoc*. In fact,

67

for all we know the cutting of the rope was not *post hoc* at all. You might as well say that my action caused yours. Or that they occurred simultaneously—and perhaps coincidentally. Hume, you know."

"Whom?"

"Forget it."

"How can I? All your *ergo* and *hoc* aside, it's obvious to me we're in this together. Linked by fate."

"Fate?"

"Yes. Linked by fate. Torn by passion. Alone with the man she never knew. Together against tempestuous odds on sub-glacial seas of indifference. Sub-glacial? No, sub-glacial will never do. But I can see the cover, can't you? Except that the neckline on this cagoule does not plunge nearly enough—in fact it doesn't plunge at all. We'll have to fix that. But you with the oars—just perfect—and that little wet curl on your forehead, gleaming in the lantern light. That's it, set the jaw, and—"

"Jen!"

"Well, it's worth considering," she trailed off. She was a bit surprised at her own silliness, given the occasion. But she supposed it might be good for morale—hers certainly, and Ronald's secretly. And somehow he had set her off.

"You know what I've been thinking?" said Ronald, sounding as if he'd been thinking it for a long time.

"What?" said Jennifer. She set herself for a new romantic revelation, or some devastating reflection on her character.

"I've been thinking this lake is the same one that Dr. Slupensky discovered today—or yesterday. You know what I mean. Which puts us under the eastern lobe, like Garth said. The crystal chamber must have been beneath the divide, just below the nunatak."

Their location was not so important to Jennifer as it was

to him. She could rely on Ronald in any conversation to trans-form feelings to information.

"So," she said, nudging the end of William's boots, "what *did* you do? After it started raining and all."

"All I *could* do," Ronald replied. "With the rope cut I was afraid to approach the edge of the schrund, since it might col-lapse at the overhang. So I scrambled up to our pillar of rock, untied what was left of the rope, and brought it back to where I had lain. There I sank my ax to the hilt and tied a bowline around the shaft. I padded the lip the best I could with my rucksack and threw down the rope, hoping there was enough to reach. Then I rapped in."

"You rappeled? With that marmot around? He could have bitten off your rope too!"

"I thought of that. And I looked for him the best I could. But it was foggy, remember? I had to risk it."

In spite of her retroactive concern, Jennifer found herself admiring him for what he had done. "And?" she said.

"And the rope reached—just. When I got to the bottom I found him bleeding, unconscious, in three inches of running water. I knew I had to get him out of *that*, no matter if his neck was broken, no matter if he was bleeding to death, because he'd die of hypothermia first. It was roomy down there—maybe eighty feet down, and I dragged him up on a dry shelf under the wall. There were a few drips from the cornice above, but he was out of the stream and out of the rain. I laid him on my parka and tried to stop the blood from his side. It didn't work—you saw my hands. As far as I could tell there were no bones broken—a miracle, considering—but not much help if he didn't stop bleeding.

"In my mind I was trying to work out how I could strap him to my back and prussik up the rope—though as long as it rained he would stay more sheltered there in the crevasse. But if I could stop the bleeding I knew that I might have to leave to get help. So I was thinking these things, holding my hands against the blood, when the rope that was hanging from my ax suddenly came down in a heap."

"You mean, the marmot chomped it?"

"I mean, the rope fell in a heap in the running water below our ledge. That's all I could directly observe. Marmot or no, same result."

Jennifer wondered what drove him to be so distressingly factual. "It must have been the marmot," she complained. "What else could it be?"

"A bad knot, a sharp edge of ice, who knows? But yes, the marmot is a distinct possibility, given its recent strange behavior."

"So you walked."

"I walked. But first I waited. The cave at the closed-off end of the schrund looked none too inviting. I hadn't been in the system before, and anyway, I didn't have a light. My headlamp was up in my pack, eighty feet of overhung ice away. It was getting dark even there in the open crevasse as night came on, and the rain wasn't stopping."

"Sounds like you in a heap of trouble, boy," Jennifer mocked.

Ronald looked hurt and stilled the oars. She knew he would need some coaxing to continue, and asked herself why she didn't keep still and let Ronald be Ronald. "Hey," she said feebly, "a joke. I'm sorry."

"Anyhow," Ronald went on quietly, "that's when Garth showed up. At first he was just a light down the tunnel as I looked in from the ice shelf. I called out as loud as I could, hoping it was your dad, or Slupensky, or someone else on the cave survey. But the light just kept floating toward me, and no one called back. When it reached the open air of the schrund, still at a distance, I made out a single figure, in a poncho or something, walking as if out for a stroll. When he got to us I saw he was wearing a long wool robe and a long white beard. He was no one I had ever seen. I said, 'Hey, we're in trouble.' He simply took my hands from William's side and held them in his own. He didn't say anything—he just looked at me—and, Jen, his eyes were unspeakably sad."

Jennifer nodded, a bit surprised at his sudden passion.

"I suppose they were dark anyway, but in the evening rain at the shadowy bottom of the crevasse, his eyes were dark as obsidian. Yes," he said, as if reflecting on the image, "obsidian."

She blessed the day he had met this man who had dislocated him into poetry.

"There's not much more to it, really. He told me his name after a while and said to me, 'What has come to be has been appointed, but woe to him who severs the heart.' He sounded sorry and matter-of-fact, not at all judgmental, if you know what I mean."

"I do know what you mean," said Jennifer. "Lady Demaris spoke like that. They're serious, aren't they, but I don't think they're out to get us. They know how to be angry without being mad. Like Mom was."

Ronald paused. Jennifer sensed he was wishing he could say the same for his dead father. That they were each partly orphaned was the secret they touched on in intimate moments.

"Anyhow," he continued, "Garth untied the rope and lifted William into his arms. Then he nodded to William's ax and simply said, 'You'll be needing that.' I hadn't noticed the ax since I'd come down the rope. It was stuck in the ice spike-first in the stream. I yanked on it, but it didn't come out. Then I yanked harder. 'On your knees first,' Garth told me. 'Then it will come.' I kneeled down in the same stream into which William had fallen, and the ax came out with a gentle pull."

"I suppose it might," Jennifer mused.

"Then I coiled up the two wet ropes—or the two parts of the wet rope—and followed Garth down the—what's that?"

"Down the what's that?"

"No, listen. Don't you hear it?"

Jennifer strained her ears past the echo of their dying voices and heard the rush of water ahead. "One of those moulins," she said. "A little shower out of the ceiling. Please row around it, James."

"It's much louder than that," said Ronald, holding the oars erect in the air like rabbit ears at full attention. "Here, Jen, put your hand in the water for a moment. That's right. Feel anything?"

She did as instructed, and felt the water purling against her outstretched hand with surprising force. In the same moment she felt the current catch the boat and launch it into the water's momentum. The noise ahead was no longer an echo.

"Hold up the light!" Ronald shouted.

In her nervousness she snatched at the lantern and held it up with such a jerk that the flame snuffed out. Ronald shouted something else, but now it was too dark to hear—at least that's how it felt. The sound of rushing water ahead redoubled and redoubled again, filling her ears like the terrible sound of glaciers calving into the ocean, something she had once seen and heard with her father from a large ship in the north. Her thought was that the Mirror Glacier was destroying itself, falling in upon the lake in bergs and slabs and monstrous pieces.

When the sound could not possibly get any louder, the boat tipped forward. Jennifer suddenly lurched from her seat and bruised her face on William's boots. She felt the boat hurtling downward, the splash of water and hiss of air against her back. Her stomach was caught up into her throat, and she waited, and waited, and waited for the impact—the moment when they would hit bottom and smash into splinters of wood and bone. No one, she reflected, would ever find them, much less recognize them if they did, and this thought turned her fear forlorn. She had read of a man discovered at the foot of a glacier some four thousand years after he had fallen into a crevasse. But she would not have even that immortality. It was little comfort to think of being rolled round in a glacial river with rocks and stones and trees.

But the obliterating impact never came. First the boat tipped left as if banking a curve on a bobsled run, and then suddenly right, so sharply that Jennifer grabbed the bench above her head, and was horrified to find that Ronald was no longer on it. Her first thought was that Ronald was overboard; lying in the loud and rushing dark, shifting this way and that as the boat plunged its course, she tried to think how she might search for him. A foolish thought, but one that told her where her heart was.

How long she raced down the black whitewater she didn't know. After a while she gave up her anxieties for herself—it was no use cringing at every turn when nothing happened, and keeping herself at a pitch of fright was too exhausting. Little by little the noise and velocity seemed to lessen, and at length she realized she was holding the bench much harder than she needed to. She found that she was quite wet, and that next to her ear there seemed to be water sloshing about in the bottom of the boat. Then the roar of the water outside the boat subsided to a gentle murmur, echoing like a dark caress. She lifted her head, slowly and cautiously in case the ceiling were low here, and righted herself on her knees in the water in the bottom of the boat. Her hands were clasped on the bench as in prayer when the boat turned a corner into thin gray light. The stream was broad and the ceiling high over steely swirls, and there in the bow she saw Ronald thrown on his back like a bug, lying on William and gripping both sides of the boat for life.

Then the cave was gone, passed like a dream, and raindrops fell on her upturned face.

8

"WHAT ARE YOU DOING down there?" asked Jennifer. "Niagara Falls on the River Styx and you decide to take a nap."

Ronald rose up out of the bow as if he were William's departing spirit. He slowly took his seat amidships by the oars, and Jennifer, still down on her knees, clasped him tightly about the waist. "You okay?" she asked more gently. "I thought you were gone. I'm glad you're not."

Ronald was still too stunned to reply, and perhaps too shy, but he welcomed the touch of her arms about him as he welcomed the born-again touch of rain. He sat quietly looking at clouds and trees and sand and river revealed in light. The river was broad, a milky gray, and calm but swift between sandy flats. He had seen this spot a hundred times from the nunatak high up on the glacier, but never before had he been here where the Amoenas River shot out from the Mirror Glacier into the forest. The stone-mottled walls of the glacier behind them were fast retreating, and the nunatak was lost in clouds. Even the giant cedar trees that anchored the shore were wrapped in mist, huddled and dark except for the flame of vine maple that sometimes ignited beneath them. This was the blessing of the world. It shone wet, and wide, and they were in it, delivered from darkness.

"Hello," said Jennifer, suddenly releasing him. "We can't let William just wallow about in the water down there. We've got ourselves a regular lake. What do you say we row to shore and find a way to dry out a bit? I'm not any too warm myself—and neither are you, by the feel of you, Ronald. We're much too wet and cold to be safe. Hypothermia, you know, killer of the disprepared." It was a first-aid slogan she liked to misquote.

Ronald agreed, and pulled at the oars till they reached an eddy by a small creek on the left-hand bank. Both of them splashed into the shallows, and with some straining they pulled the boat up onto the sand and lifted William out of the bow. He felt dangerously sodden in their arms, so Ronald dragged him heels down toward the edge of the wood while Jennifer gathered the blankets and ropes and lantern and pack, and looked for a way to secure the boat. There was nothing at hand to tie it to, and she couldn't push it any farther from the river herself, so she simply left it where it was, stuffed everything into the generous pack, and hurried up the beach after Ronald.

It was still raining.

She caught up to him at the edge of the trees, and lifted William's sandy heels over the brush and into the quiet, the rainless hush of the old-growth forest. Here cedars grew that were girthed like ancient pillars of a temple. High above, thick branches wove a canopy to protect them from the worst of the wet. On the forest floor grew clumps of fern, but little else. Unobstructed they hauled William across the duff until they came to a fire-scarred hollow within the base of a particularly large red cedar some ways into the wood.

Once inside they found the hollow to really be a snug dry room, large enough for all of them to stretch out in comfort. They laid William down on his wet wool blanket until Jennifer found two drier ones in the very bottom of Chambers' pack. There was also bread and a canister of soup inside the blankets—and just as important, candles and flint. Ronald collected an armload of branches and just at the entrance started a fire from dry shavings and dead twigs that Jennifer had gathered within the room. They shed boots and socks, and found various blackened knots and niches from which to hang steaming sweaters and parkas, and sat on their blankets next to the fire and felt their fingers and toes come to life.

Jennifer broke off half a loaf, and it tasted rough and sweet in their mouths. The soup they kept at the edge of the fire, and when it was as hot again as it had been in Chambers' kettle, they drank huge portions down in turn, and felt as warmed within as without. Jennifer had a wonderful feeling of safety, and home. She wondered if it would be like this should they really marry.

But when they had grown quite comfortable, they realized they had forgotten to tend to William's welfare. "He's not just a dead body, you know," Jennifer scolded.

Ronald removed the boots and socks and loosened the clothing to let it dry. He checked the wounds and found no discharge. William still breathed peacefully, apparently in a deep sleep.

"Do we save some for him?" Jennifer said, holding out the soup and bread.

"Maybe," said Ronald, "but not now. If he sleeps for a week, I think we should let him."

"A week!" said Jennifer. "We'll be rowing this river for a week?"

"Well," said Ronald, "it's a day or two to the gorge anyhow, if it's the same one I've seen on the map. I don't know exactly where in the gorge this Tower of Otium is supposed to be—where Garth says we are to rest. And how long it will take to get to the sea is anyone's guess. You've been on top of the North Queen, right? That's the highest, and you can just glimpse the ocean from there, a glimmer of it anyway, when there's no slash burning and the air is clear. It's a ways, Jennifer."

He paused for a moment. "Finishing the survey might have been easier."

This stung in her ears. It was as if to say, *If you hadn't forgotten the data book, Jennifer, we'd never be on this impossible trip.* But that was the marmot's fault, when you thought about it, as was William's fall in the schrund. Though Ronald didn't have to go lunging after the book in the first place. And it *was* rather clumsy of him to slice the rope. All she'd done was to pick a beautiful and unusual flower—something anyone might have intended. And a good thing too, for without the elixir that Lady Demaris had squeezed from the rose, William might have been dead by now. Jennifer realized that she was really the heroine in this mess Ronald had created. But she would keep in temper and not allow herself to gloat or take offense.

"You'd like to finish the survey, wouldn't you, Ronald?" It was an echoing tactic she'd learned in a psychology class.

"Well, of course," he faltered.

"For science?"

"For science."

"Gwen says it's just for the dam."

"Well," said Ronald, "not *just* for the dam."

"But we wouldn't be here if it weren't for the dam, would we, Ronald? I mean, that's where the money comes from, right?"

"I suppose. In this case, anyway."

"And that's the way it always is. Science is knowledge. Knowledge is power. Power pollutes. Power destroys. Power is always power against. In our world, on merry middle earth, science is the slut of industry. Either that or the whore of war."

"Jen!" He would have been much less offended if she had slandered some person in particular. As it was, she was violating something sacred.

For Jennifer's part, she was sorry she had spoken, but as

she was playing the heroine, she could not bring herself to apologize.

Ronald drew a deep breath. "Speaking of science—"

"Which we were," Jennifer affirmed.

"Speaking of science," he began again, "I should mention something I just saw—or didn't see. The little stream where we pulled out the boat—that's the one that comes off the saddle near Chambers Lake. There should be a stream gauge—a little orange tower—just above it on the river. It's the one that Roscoe has to hike down to once a week. I've never been with him, and you haven't either, but I know what it looks like and where it is. And it's not there."

"Washed away?"

"Possibly, but there hasn't been any flooding to speak of. This is the first hard rain of the season, and the glacier release has been pretty even except for the normal fluctuations of day and night."

"So what you're saying is that we've got—"

"—an anomaly, Jen. And I've got half a mind to hike back up to the saddle from here and report it—in camp." As he said the word he remembered that he would be more likely to find a cabin. And if anyone were there at all, they would probably send him right back here with Jennifer to continue their unscientific appointed task. If he ever hoped to finish his survey, he first had to begin their quest.

He did not correct himself out loud, but merely lapsed into forlorn silence. "What time is it anyway?" he finally complained. "I left my watch in my rucksack."

"You should ask me," said Jennifer slyly, looking about the inner walls of the burnt trunk as if for a clue. "There's no clock in the forest. In fact, I don't know if it's morning or afternoon, do you? No matter, though." She stood up and struck a thespian pose, arms outspread in front of the fire. "I like this place," she proudly declaimed, "and willingly could waste my time in it."

"You what?" said Ronald. "*This* place?"

> *"And this our life, exempt from public haunt,*
> *Finds tongues in trees, books in the running brooks,*
> *Sermons in stone, and good in everything."*

She exulted in every word as it came.

Ronald still looked confused.

"Shakespeare," she said. "The Forest of Arden. I had to read it aloud in class, and before that, with my mom at home. It stuck, I guess. Almost as good as Shelley. Mary, that is."

"I don't know about books and sermons," Ronald said, "but I'd like to check on that stream gauge, just to be sure."

He peered past the fire and held his hand out the entrance. "I think it's stopped. At least it's not raining as hard as it was. I'll run down to the river for just a bit and come right back."

"If you want," said Jennifer. "Just don't fall in or anything." She heard much more concern in her voice than she thought she had intended, and realized it was as much for herself as it was for him. She did not relish the prospect of being left by herself in the wilderness. It is one thing to feel the lonely solace of open spaces on alpine slopes, and quite another to be tucked deep down in a dripping forest by the icy surge of a glacial stream. She felt entangled and enfolded here, far back in the sinister ply of the non-human. "Good in everything" indeed. Fine enough for on-campus, or for whatever tame place the Forest of Arden might have been. But Blake was more like it—crazy Blake with his

> *Tyger Tyger burning bright*
> *In the forests of the night.*

That was the forest not as she liked it but as it was.

She felt almost ashamed of these darkwood thoughts, so uncongenial to the immanence of the earth goddess. But in the moments that Ronald put on his boots and recollected his sweater and parka, she had to admit these *were* her thoughts. Too embarrassed to give or receive a parting kiss for such a brief errand, she watched him step around the fire and over the rich rust floor of the forest, out through a corridor of trees till he merged with the gloom. She caught one last glimpse of his innocent head against the crimson explosion of vine maple, and then he was gone, perhaps crossing the sand to the river's edge. She watched the spot in the vine maple for a sentimental length of time, then sighed and added more wood to the fire.

She turned to William and tried to breathe as slowly and calmly as he did. "I love him, you know. Every bit as much as Gwen loves you." At the thought of Gwen she allowed herself to softly cry and wondered where her friend might be and what she could know of what had happened. "You have to get better," she instructed him. "You're going to be a father soon, and I don't think you'll want to sleep through *that*. You'd be the first, anyhow." The thought made her laugh, but only in a sad sort of way.

She fell to musing by the fire, shifted her boots away from the flames, and curled up on top of her blanket and under Ronald's. Staying up all night in a glacier cave had not improved her wakefulness, and though she wished to wait for Ronald's return before falling asleep, she proved herself no different from any of the ten virgins in the parable, and drifted off.

When Jennifer woke, the fire had collapsed in embers and the forest was very nearly dark. She heard the breath of William beside her, as dead and calm as air from a bellows—and no other breath besides.

"Ronald," she whispered. She sat up. "Ronald!"

No one.

Just to be sure, she stoked the fire and found in the glancing light of the flames that Ronald certainly was not there. She had no idea how long she'd slept, but two ideas, both unthinkable, about his absence—accident and outright desertion. And a third idea—murder most foul—when she considered that loathsome marmot.

She knew from experience that out in the open next to the river it still would not be quite dark, and prepared the lantern to help her follow Ronald's tracks. She threw a few more boughs on the fire to ensure a beacon for her return, and set off in her newly dried boots and socks. She felt the air quiet and cool about her face, a presence between the living columns of bark and heartwood. In a few moments she reached a thicket of vine maple, struggled through it, and found herself on the sand near the river—not too near, for the beach was wide, testimony to the glacier's power of swift release. The roar of the river was thick and steady upon her ears, and the clouds swayed low, blowing eastward.

On her left she heard the thin rush of the tributary that came from the saddle, and she followed it in the failing light to the corner of shore where brook met river. There were bootprints here, partly melted by the rain. For a moment her gaze was distracted by a parting of the clouds upstream that framed the face of the evening star in the twilight sky. Then she took in what was not there—no boat, and no fresh tracks leading back to the forest.

"Ronald!" she cried. The name was swallowed by the sound of the river. Even as she watched, the water scooped the sand from her feet and hurried on.

9

WHEN RONALD STEPPED OUT of the woods to the sand sometime that morning or afternoon, he glanced upshore and down through the misty rain for the orange-towered gauge he knew in his heart he would not see. Only as an afterthought, as he came close to the river's edge, did he think to check on Chambers' boat. He reached the water a bit upcurrent from where they had left it, and sure enough, when he looked downstream, there it was beached on the spit of sand that brought the creek and river together. The boat looked secure for the time being, but was perilously close to the water. Though the glacier would not release its afternoon melt, the new rainfall might cause the river to rise even so, and Ronald determined to pull the boat farther onto the shore if he could.

For a moment he wondered at Jennifer for leaving it so close to the water, but part of him realized that *he* had left the boat as well, so he excused her at least to the level of complicity. He was deep in this disposition of blame, and perhaps forty yards away from the boat, when it inexplicably started to give—not the boat but the shore, and not inexplicably, given the daily force of the current, and not just the current, given the glimpse he suddenly had of a mountainous marmot trenching the sand from under the stern. It fixed him with an ashen eye and tore at the sand undergirding the boat with doglike fervor.

For a moment Ronald stood still in surprise. Then he flew

at the boat and the marmot with all his scientific strength, and partway there tripped over a rock, diving as swans are said to do upon his chest, where he choked on the loss of his own wind. From his prone and breathless vantage point he watched as the boat sank away with the sand and slowly slipped out into the water. For a moment it hovered near the shore, and then the current caught the prow and gently whirled it past the mouth of the small creek. The marmot stood on the broken bank and glared at Ronald as if to say, *I dare you to act.* Then it splashed through the tributary creek and swung across the beach to the trees. For a fat marmot, it could gallop like a buffalo.

Ronald took the dare and stood up gasping. He stumbled ahead, splashed through the creek behind the marmot, and, feeling the return of his breath, paused to consider whether he should go after the boat, the marmot, or Jennifer. Revenge, and the marmot, was his first impulse; and then solace, and Jennifer. Heroism, and certain drowning, was not really a live option, until suddenly the boat strayed into a shoreside eddy, underneath a half-buried log that was not so very far downstream, and began to loop in a lazy twirl tantalizingly close to the sand.

That made up his mind, and he dashed down the sand, socks squishing inside his boots, carefully leaping the snags and boulders in his path. He reached the log and the lucky eddy just as the boat swung past his reach. He stood on tiptoe, waiting for it to orbit again, but this time the boat slipped back into the waiting current, bouncing stern, then prow against the log and then sailing down the river again in midstream. He had no intention of diving in after it, but what happened once might happen again, and he hurried down the sandy shore, hoping the boat would meet again with a helpful eddy or obstruction.

It easily outdistanced him on the swift strong current, and

soon disappeared around a bend in the barren drizzle. He
stopped in momentary despair, but then considered he could
not know what lay around the bend in the river unless he went
to see. And so he did, keeping up a dogged spirit, and rounded
the bend in time to watch the boat fade away around the next
one. But that bend too might hold serendipities, and so he continued, and continued, and continued, till he did not see the
boat anymore, and was wetter from perspiration within his
parka than from the fading drizzle without. After a while he
lost the strength and urgency to run, and settled into a fatal-
istic walk, telling himself at every turn to give it up and go
back to Jennifer, but somehow not doing so. The body has its
own inertia, even when the mind has other plans. And so it
was that Ronald kept walking, long after he had given up on
reason and hope.

What stopped him finally, long after the rain had ceased,
was the thunder of rapids that came to him from a narrow
rocky defile ahead. The beach was pinched off on either side
by mossy bluffs, bright green and water slick, that crowded in
against the river and shot it through a boiling slot. The river
water, to this point a milky gray with the glacier flour of ice-
ground stone, was thrown into raging columns of white that
slammed into a fern-decked wall and exploded off in a sudden
turn. Ronald walked to the end of the sand and looked down
the Charybdis of whitewater to where it smashed into the
Scylla of the ferny wall. The boat, of course, was nowhere in
sight, and he reasonably concluded it was shivered into a thousand wood chips, rather like slurry in a pulpwood mill, circling
in eddies below the rapid like a band of angels hovering next
to the Son of Man lest he dash his foot against a stone. For a
moment he was grateful the marmot had launched the boat as
it had. There was no way they could have survived the rapid,
and the current above it was so swift that they may not have

been able to beach the boat before being swallowed down this throat of unbearably dark white noise.

He stood mesmerized at the head of the rapid for quite some time, wondering what he might do next. There was no scrambling over the mossy bluffs—they were too steep and slippery. And having come this far in pursuit of the boat, he didn't much relish the idea of returning to Jennifer empty-handed. He had reached an impasse of mind and place.

Eventually he found himself watching a slate-gray bird—a water ouzel—dipping about where the last smooth stretch of river current plunged into the violence of the narrows. Heedless of the chaos—or perhaps heeding it most of all—the ouzel hopped and flung itself this way and that, sometimes diving beneath the water to re-emerge, unscathed and unruffled, at the very edge of the white upheaval. The more he watched, the more Ronald wondered that the bird was so well able to thrive on the boundary of death. *Be careful*, he wanted to call out, and each time the ouzel disappeared, he sympathetically held his breath until it resurfaced. As if conscious of this sympathy, each time it popped back out of the water the bird was a little closer to Ronald. And then it was perched on the shore at his feet, shaking itself in a fit of flutter. Ronald now saw it was smaller than a robin, larger than a sparrow, a plump bird with a stubby tail.

"So you're safe, are you?" he said aloud. "I'm glad for that." He surprised himself with his sentimentality. At least that's what he would have called it before.

The ouzel looked at him steadily, dipping on its legs like a nervous courtier making a series of short awkward bows. "*Bzeet!*" it said.

"Aren't you cold?" Ronald asked. "It's drier out of the water, you know."

As if taking his suggestion, the ouzel bounced past Ronald's feet and stopped on the other side of him. Then it hopped farther, closer to the forest, and halted and looked and hopped again. At the very edge of the big trees—hemlocks, not cedars—and up against the mossy wall, it paused and eyed him once more, dipping and bowing as politely as ever. Then it disappeared into the green world.

Ronald stood looking after it, wishing somehow the bird were back. Suddenly it was, watching him from beneath the fronds of sword fern at the forest edge. *"Bzeet-bzeet-bzeet!"* Then it darted back into the woods.

In his mind there echoed the voice of commission:

The song of the ouzel lead thee aright.

The words seemed alarmingly slight things to trust. But he sensed that he might, and the possibility filled him with strange exhilaration. He paused, and then, without quite knowing why, he followed the bird into the trees. Waist-deep in ferns, he did not see its shape at first. The ground was steep here, hard against the rising bluff, and he had to peer upward to catch sight of the ouzel again, resting against the firm gray trunk of a stolid hemlock. It paused there as if waiting for him, and when he caught up to it, took off again.

And so they pursued the journey in stages, the bird darting effortlessly, and Ronald pulling himself upward, staining his hands with fistfuls of fern. After a while the hill began to ease to an angle of something closer to human repose, and Ronald was able to make his way unaided by ferns, though still crouching on all fours. The duff in his hands was deep and rich, musty with the millennia of hemlock which had given their lives, their fallen bodies, for each succeeding generation. The air was quiet away from the river, and unexpectedly Ronald felt a sense of home here, deep beneath the giant trees and lacy needles, somewhere lost in a dim damp canyon, pawing the earth like a lumbering bear. He had known such surprising contentment before—the sheer pleasure at times of standing on the nunatak amidst the swell and spill of ice. It was a pleasure unrelated to whether he completed the survey of the day or not. It was the simple happiness of belonging, of being there, a participant in something ancient, more grand and good than he could imagine. And now in the forest it was like this too.

But the feeling was fleeting, impermanent as an ouzel in space. Soon the slope eased again, and Ronald was able to pick his way along upright. When the ground became nearly level he suddenly lost sight of the ouzel and crashed through the ferns in a bit of a panic. Then, quite simply, he found himself standing on a comfortable trail leading left and right, parallel to the river below. And just to the right of him, bobbing obediently, the ouzel waited on the path. Then it turned eastward, downstream, and Ronald followed.

He was delighted of course to find a trail, but dismayed to be going still farther from Jennifer. It seemed dimmer in the forest than when he had entered, and he sensed that evening was coming on. And why, he wondered, was he trusting a bird? But he went on in spite of himself, thinking the trail might very well lead back to the river below the rapid. It was perhaps too late to return anyway, and this might be his last chance to find the boat, should it still exist.

As he had hoped, the trail after coursing level for a ways began to descend and finally to switchback down through the forest. The ouzel fluttered faithfully on, and as the woods began to grow truly dusky Ronald started to hear the river once again. Then he could see it, just to the right of him through the trees, under limbed curtains of pale green lichen, and he plowed through the ferns again until he regained the familiar flood-bared sandy shore.

The river and riverside looked quite empty under the deepening evening clouds. He felt all alone, and more than foolish,

and suddenly realized he no longer had a clue as to where the
ouzel was. For all he knew it was still on the trail. He turned
to enter the woods again, tired beyond discouragement, and
knew he must find a place to rest. He had just touched the
edge of the ferns when the bird alighted on his sleeve and
announced itself. *"Bzeet-bzeet!"* Just as quickly it hopped away
down the beach.

"You again," Ronald said, disguising relief as exasperation.
He summoned the strength to follow the ouzel once again,
wondering how long this could last.

Not long. In less than a minute the ouzel stopped in a natural cove, split off by a rock from the river, and came to rest
on the silhouette of Chambers' boat, calmly afloat and completely intact on still waters. Ronald ran up and burst into
tears. It was so unlike him, but he did not care.

He carefully reached to the prow from the sand and pulled
it ashore, all the lovely, smooth-knit heft of its marvelous
entirety. He dragged it well up onto the beach and smiled at
the bird in the gathering dark. The ouzel only bowed, of
course. Ronald pulled the boat all the way to the forest edge
and with his last strength tipped it over against a log well-
banked with ferns.

He looked upstream to the parted clouds and the evening
star. "Good night," he said, and crawled inside.

10

It was dark when Jennifer listlessly returned to the forest. It seemed clear that Ronald had deserted her. But how? And why? How terribly estranged he must have felt to abandon her in so desperate a way. She reviewed in her mind each playful insult that had passed her lips in his company, and regretted them all. It was her fault.

And then it was not her fault—it was his. No sooner did Jennifer slap face-first into something solid and wooden in the dark than she became victim in love as well. How stupid of her to promise herself to a man hardly human, a robotic piece of empiricism who was only happy when scoping out little orange flags on a glacier but incapable of admiring the view, natural or feminine, outside a theodolite. She would . . . She would . . . She did not know what things she'd do, but they would be the terrors of the earth.

And so she repented and threatened by turns, paying very little attention really to where she was going, letting the dim broad trunks slip by, and occasionally tripping over a root or mashing into a clump of fern or devil's club, the sting of which only rearoused her feelings of fury, should they have temporarily abated. Not taking care where she went, it soon followed, when she stopped to think, that she did not know where she had come. In the back of her mind she supposed she had been looking for the fire at the door of the tree, but she saw none now, and realized she had been on the beach quite long enough for the flames to have burned very low. Her sense of responsibility for William began to displace her penitent and outraged sense of romantic loss, and she stood in one place for a long time, gathering her breath and thoughts. She listened for the voice of the river, but it was faraway and indistinct, no closer before than behind her.

She stumbled this way and that for a while, hoping to catch sight of the embers. She even called out William's name before she remembered how silly that was. But her aimless sorties were no use. She was lost, and would stay so till morning. Not knowing what else to do, she burrowed into the damp and duff against the roots of a great cedar and, covering herself with bark and ferns, curled up with her hood round her face to try and get some sleep.

Which she didn't, of course, not at least till the night was far gone. For hours she listened to small things scurrying past her ears. Little bugs crawled onto her face from time to time, and once, she thought, something wet and soft, perhaps a toad. Her bones ached with cold and fatigue, and her stomach gouged itself with hunger.

Somewhere towards morning a breeze must have sprung up overhead, for the tree beside her began to groan as if in sadness. She must have been listening to the sound of it when she fell asleep, for in her dreams the tree began to speak with her, except it wasn't the tree exactly, nor a disembodied tongue neither, but the arboreal essence of it, a walking thing, tall and lean and incredibly mournful, standing before her with bark-browed eyes. Its feet were crumbling into the earth, falling apart in shreds and chunks like frostbitten flesh.

"What think you of this bondage to decay, daughter of God?" He must have seen a look of confusion on Jennifer's face, for he hastened to explain, "I am hoping you may be revealed as such. Subjected to futility, you may think. But also, remember, subjected in hope. The river gives its life for me, and I shall give my life for the river. Gladly I shall lay it down."

It shifted on its roots as if to scrutinize her better. "Do not fear. I and all my brothers are with you, insofar as you become your liberty. The freedom of the river is yours, and the freedom you gain shall be the river's. Until then we groan, daughter of God. There are pangs of birth too deep for words. Take care, take joy. Farewell."

And with these last words he clapped his hands, and a rain of bark broke off from his arms and fell to earth. She awoke; it was dark. Jennifer had the strangest feeling that a huge branch had crashed to the ground from high overhead, but there would be no way of knowing for sure, even in the light of morning. She shivered, cold and sore in her nest, and pondered the figure in her dream. She had read of the spirits of trees before. Dryads in Ovid (though these were female, as she remembered), and gentle emanations of the goddess herself in the poetry of the health food store. But this tree seemed neither god nor goddess. When he had called her daughter of God, he did not seem to think himself her earthly father. He appeared rather grand, to be sure, but only in a decrepit sort of way. He was hoping for something and hoping in something—her, in a way, but mostly something or someone beyond her. God perhaps. That loathsome piece of patriarchal obsolescence that Ronald quietly used to invoke in the days before he had begun to study with her father.

She turned and returned her troubled thoughts until she slept and dreamed again. This time she was walking in the forest, the same one in which she lay. It was morning. Shafts of sunlight played upon the rain-fresh floor, and she quickly found the hollow tree. The fire was out, but wisps of smoke still rose from the embers. She stepped around the ashes to the door, hoping to find William at least and perhaps even Ronald. But what she saw was the mounded bulk of the hoary marmot, gnawing at something, worrying it like a dog at a bone. Instinctively she cried and gave it a vicious kick, but it hardly moved. It looked up and glared and bared its teeth, and she kicked it again, and again, and again, and finally it galloped into the forest. In the place where it had done its work were the grisly remains of William's feet, the heel of each one quite chewed off and bleeding, bleeding, into the ground. As if he had not bled enough.

She woke up weeping, pale sunlight in her face. Her body was shivering all over from cold, or grief, or perhaps both. It was at times like these that she longed for her mother, the touch of her hand on her waking brow, the word of welcome to the new day. *In bondage to decay. Subjected to futility. Subjected in hope.* She repeated the dryad's phrases in her mind, and began to sense how widely they applied.

"Still asleep, dear?"

Jennifer rose as if from the grave, bark and fern sliding off her clothes as she sat up. She saw standing beside her, stranger than dream, the smock-clad figure of Lady Demaris.

"There, you are awake. Peace, be quiet, I cannot stay. I bring bread for your journey and words of hope. Ronald shall return, and you must return him to your love. William must away and you must find him, but first press on to the Tower of Otium. Where the water is white, you are most in the arms of my sweet sister. Trust her care. I must take my leave to the land of shadows and thence to the middle of the Western Sea. We shall meet again at the Western strand, or even at the Tower, when all is well."

She offered her hand, and Jennifer clasped it and arose, brushing off the beard of earth that clung so closely. She was about to ask Lady Demaris to repeat and explain what she had just said, but the woman pulled her quickly in tow through forest and sunlight, over the ferny banks and gardens, past red-pulp explosions of coral root, all as fresh as in her dream. Soon they came to the hollow tree, guarded by its wisp of smoke, and Lady Demaris gestured within like the angel at the empty tomb. And it was empty. Jennifer stooped and looked inside and quickly saw that William was minus not only his heels but also, as it were, himself. There were the blankets, there was the pack. There, even, were his boots and socks.

"Where have you taken him?" Jennifer demanded.

"Child," Lady Demaris replied, "it is not I that would take him, but would keep him. Look here," she said, and pointed to the churn of duff outside. "These are the tracks of many horses that belong to the servants of the great El Ai. He himself is slave to the spirit of my sad sister, the Lady Lira, worshiped now in that desert kingdom as Lady Lyra, we are told. For her revenge and for his need, the need of El Ai, the marmot has come and the body is taken."

"The body?" said Jennifer. "You mean—"

"Until his deliverance, until his revealing, William is hardly anything else."

"I—I'm so sorry. I know last night I should have . . ." She trailed off.

"Should have. Should have," Lady Demaris said. There was a trace of bitterness in her serenity. "To only know *should have* is to be in bondage."

"To decay?" added Jennifer.

"Yes," she answered.

"Futility," they both said together.

Lady Demaris reached out and stroked Jennifer's brow. "And hope, child."

They passed a moment in intimate silence, and Jennifer wept, much as she just had minutes ago upon awaking.

"Now gather your things," Lady Demaris said in time. "I will set you on your way."

Jennifer obediently folded the blankets and boots into the pack, and Lady Demaris handed her new loaves of bread. They broke one together and ate in quiet, listening to the varied shrill of a morning thrush.

Jennifer found herself studying the gentle face, the strong green eyes, the rich brown hair with admiration. "Lady Demaris," she finally said, "are you—a goddess?"

Lady Demaris laughed like a spring in an alpine meadow, tossing her head in genuine merriment. "If I am," she said, "it is only with a very small g. It is he that made us, and not we ourselves. And though we call him *he*, he is not a man, not really. But, oh dear, not woman neither. Male nor female—something, *someone* much better than that. Purest Being, Living Water, closer to us than the air in our lungs or the blood in our veins. I consist in him, but I am not he, and he is not I. You can meet him here; he is completely in this place, but not of it, not at all."

"At the Tower of Otium—there perhaps?"

"You can look, my daughter. He blows with the wind. And with him, sometimes, so do I–for I did not think to see you so soon. It is important to find him where we are found."

Lady Demaris turned her head. "But see who comes to find you now, seeking for the woman within and the woman without."

Jennifer looked and saw Ronald striding far off in the trees. He did not yet see them. She called his name and jumped up and ran to where he was. His face was pale and his hair a damp mess. She felt a terrible need to recover and take care of him, and when she reached him they fell into an awkward embrace, each one mumbling apologies.

"But come here, look," Jennifer said, pulling him by the arm to the tree. "Look who's here, and look who isn't."

But there by the tree where little birds hopped among the crumbs, it was all *isn't*.

"But she was just here," Jennifer complained.

"Who?" asked Ronald.

11

IT WAS JUST MID-MORNING, and cloudy again, when Jennifer and Ronald arrived back at his hermitage under the overturned boat. Their trail, which passed quite close to the tree from which William was taken, had been full of hoofprints pointed downstream.

"Well," said Ronald, pushing over the boat, "at least they spared us one problem. We could never have brought him all the way down the trail ourselves. Think about it. We might have woven a stretcher out of our ropes, but one of those takes at least four people to carry any distance. A blessing in disguise, as Dad used to say."

"If we get him back, that is," said Jennifer. Ronald's assessment struck her as the least bit callous. She had been more than relieved that the boat was found, that Ronald was safe, and that she herself was unforsaken, and had smothered him all the way down the trail with tears and heartfelt resolutions, but now that they stood by the boat once more on the wide and sandy bank of the river, she felt the irritability of fear, wondering what the journey might bring. She had never rowed a river before, and to her knowledge neither had Ronald. They had friends at school who invited them from time to time on rafting trips, but she always had to work at the store, and Ronald always chose to study. Over the summers they had learned their way around on a glacier, but in the moment their axes had changed into oars she knew they were launched into unknown waters. And there was no choosing. With William or now without, their charge was to float to the Tower of Otium. After hearing from Ronald about the rapid their boat had navigated without them, she hoped they would be alive when they got there.

But what she voiced was a milder fear. "This Tower of Otium—do you think we'll know it when we see it?"

"Beats me," said Ronald, shrugging his shoulders. "It's in the gorge somewhere."

That word *gorge* did not set well with Jennifer at all. She imagined black walls rising sheer from miles of boiling cataracts, with no way out but down and through, and that way quite impossible. "Well," she said simply, "I imagine we'll find it."

She helped him pull the boat to the cove where he had caught it the evening before. With William gone, they stowed the pack in the bow for ballast. Ronald offered her the oars, but she declined and took her seat in the stern again. Ronald sat down facing her, then changed his mind and turned completely around on the bench.

"I like to see what's coming," he said. "You bail." He pointed to a wooden bucket under her seat that Jennifer had not noticed before. "When the water comes in, you scoop it out. I'm afraid you'll be as busy as I am." With that he stroked them out of the cove and into the current, and with face set downstream poised the oars for what might come.

And to their delight, what came first was the water ouzel, skimming across the water from shore to land precisely on the tip of the bow, dipping and bobbing like the movable figurehead that it was.

"Is that—" said Jennifer, and Ronald nodded vigorously, as if asking her to please be quiet.

"He's so cute!" she gushed.

But before she could satisfy her interest, a steady roar

began to gather in her ears. Half rising to peer downstream, Ronald began to pull on the oars to slow them down. The boat suddenly turned at an angle, and Jennifer saw the river ahead crushing itself on a pile of snags and logs in midstream. Around it the water churned white and dropped away on either side.

"Left!" she called, thinking she saw safe passage there. "No, right!"

Ronald was trying, she could tell, to gauge the same choices. But each side pounded a terrifying violence, and it was impossible to look over the brink in either direction. They would have to commit themselves very soon, for Ronald could not stay them completely, and if they kept on course they would smash into the pile of debris. It seemed an unheroic way to go, twisted under a snarl of timber on a cold and lonely stretch of river. But then, she reflected, most ways probably were. She would have to accept the end she got.

It was then that the ouzel abandoned ship, flitting across the gathering noise until it reached the end of a snag on the right-hand side of the logjam. It bobbed there as if nodding to them, then dove out of sight down into the turbulence.

"Ronald!" she called, and pointed where the bird had gone. She felt the boat turn after it and wished she could somehow help as Ronald flailed at the oars. She could tell he wasn't sure whether he should push with the current or pull against it. The choice soon became academic. Very swiftly they bore down on the pile of logs and veered right on a cushion of water around the snag where the ouzel had stopped. The bow plunged into a caldron of foam and then nosed its way—sedately, she thought, for all the raging and plowing of water about them—past a fall-decked tier of logs on each side. Then they swirled in a boiling eddy, and the bow swung under one edge of a curtain of water. It stopped and staggered beneath the influx.

"Bail!" screamed Ronald, and he pulled the lefthand oar from its lock and jammed the blade against the log that hung over the bow. Even as he strained against the face of the fall she felt the foam flood over her boots. She scooped the water, but it deepened by the instant. The boat was not moving.

And then it was, inching out from under the fall in response to Ronald's might and main. Then they were free, and the boat drifted down the frothy wake quite nearly submerged. Jennifer redoubled her efforts with the bailing bucket and hoped against hope she could clear the boat before another rapid sank them. Ronald, of course, was rowing for shore, but he might as well have been sailing an anvil until, after a good ten minutes, Jennifer had managed to empty out much of the water. He reached a sandspit next to a tributary stream and ground the boat out of the river.

Jennifer, exhausted, slumped in the stern, her boots still resting in the ice-cold bilge. "That ouzel of yours," she panted. "I don't know."

Ronald was silent. "When you were bailing," he quietly said, "I looked back. The other side was worse—a sheer drop, onto more sharp snags. I think he brought us the best way, Jen. Maybe with practice we'll get better." He smiled sheepishly.

"You really are trusting that bird, aren't you?" As she said it the ouzel reappeared, landing on the bucket in her hands. It looked at her and sang out a melodic triumph: *bzeet! bzeet! bzeet-bzeet-bzeet!*

"Now that you mention it," Ronald said, "yes."

The rest of the day went according to the pattern they had now established—not at all a smooth pattern, but soon enough a predictable one. The ouzel rode bobbing atop the prow as they coursed the current of milky gray past sand, past snags, past thickets of browning and yellowing alder, past aching crimson of vine maple and towering stands of cedar and hemlock, and over this living, changing shore the full-bellied clouds that hung dark and low and always threatened to rain but didn't. Then a roar up ahead, gathering to a solemn greatness, not thunder in the sky but thunder in the waters, and then the sight of a logjam, or a fern-decked gorge, or a maze of boulders suffused in white, and off the ouzel would scoot from the bow to mark safe passage, and Ronald would pull against the current until he saw where the bird had gone. Then the release to the chosen path, the whirling through foam past snags and rocks, and the boiling of eddies, the sudden slap of spray from the bow that caught them hard and open-mouthed, the tug of water in the bailing bucket that made Jennifer's arms and shoulders ache, and then, if they were frightened and wet enough, and if Ronald were able, a brief landing to put things to rights and to reconsider where they had been.

Sometimes they had to wring out their clothes, and more than once they were thrown from their benches and almost toppled overboard. But the path of the ouzel proved always barely safe enough, and by late afternoon, shivering and wet, they had covered many miles of river.

The shore had grown more generally rocky, and the cedar and hemlock now hugged the river in dark comfort, spreading their boughs out over the boat and knuckling their roots down into the water. The river itself had changed its gray to a green translucence and bore on its surface the scarlet leaves of the vine maple and the pale yellow of fading alder, whirling downstream like Pharaoh's horsemen caught unawares in the closing sea.

They had beached themselves in a tiny cove and were even thinking of making camp when a shaft of sunlight pierced the clouds and bathed them in its sudden warmth. All of a sudden their shady nook hard under the trees looked adequate, yes—a bearable place to spend the night—but the sun on the water brought promise of better haven down the river, and without their knowing it, convinced them their bones held strength and succor for one more go. Ronald felt a glorious second wind, the way he did when the fog cleared away from the nunatak some afternoons and left the ice in sudden splendor.

Jennifer, feeling the same quickened hope, clambered back into the boat and struck a pose that included Ronald as her fellow ancient mariner. "That which we are, we are!" she cried.

> *"One equal temper of heroic hearts*
> *Made weak by time and fate, but strong in will*
> *To strive, to seek, to find, and not to yield."*

She held up her hand as if fisting a sword, and the ouzel promptly landed on it and left in her grip a pile of droppings. "To your post!" she ordered. "Thirty lashes for the scurvy lookout."

Ronald laughed for the first time since—well, in a long time—and Jennifer marveled at their delight. They very easily could have been drowned twenty times over that day, and there was no guarantee they would succeed on this the twenty-first attempt. Yet they went, finally, in howling good humor, and all she knew was that it finally felt right. So what if Ulysses sank to his death past the Straits of Gibraltar? He and his men knew the best secrets before they got there, and that was enough. As she looked with pride at Ronald guiding the boat with the oars, dipping them no less deftly now than the ouzel flew and dipped itself, she gloried in the strength of their weakness. Subjected in hope, she glimpsed an end to their momentary light affliction and knew for a fact that living was good.

The sunbeam multiplied itself from the west into a sudden sheet of light, shining under the edge of the clouds and setting the river all aglint as if streaked with fire from within. The mossy shore gained definition of new green glory, and each lichened tree trunk slipping by now stood apart in the thisness of its new creation. In Jennifer's eyes each plank of their boat showed grainy luster, the ouzel fairly shone on the bow, and Ronald's neck and jacketed shoulders belonged to the gods. It was a moment she never could have planned for. She remembered the advice of Lady Demaris: "It is important to find him where we are found." *So this is the presence,* Jennifer thought. *Not what it is like, but what it is.*

She was so caught up in the vision of the moment that she scarcely heard the approaching rapid. She felt Ronald pull hard against the current before she saw why—the thundering line of standing waves that reached entire from shore to shore. Instinctively she looked for the ouzel to dart ahead, marking the way they had come to trust. But strangely enough, the bird perched still—as still as an ouzel can, anyway—bobbing its respects on the bow.

Ronald could not hold them long, and they took the first wave head on, shipping a huge cold wall of water and plowing through to a bigger ahead. The ouzel had bounced itself high in the air to avoid the splash, but alighted now on Ronald's shoulder as if to say, "Your guess is as good as mine."

The second wave sent Ronald tumbling backwards into Jennifer's lap, and would have sent her overboard had Ronald not already landed on top of her. Once over the wave they both pitched forward, tangled together between the benches and half submerged in the water sloshing about on the boards. All that Jennifer could see were the handles of the oars tearing back and forth, and the courteous ouzel, perched again on Ronald's shoulder and looking at her hard in the eye. Her body felt a shock, and a sheet of spray, as if they had staved themselves on a rock, and then the boat whirled about, and the light turned, and finally the ouzel flew off.

In that moment Jennifer felt the entire boat grow suddenly weightless, lifted, it seemed, from the pounding water. Then she knew a soft sinking sensation, which ought to have grown faster but didn't. The oars were still, and the air was full of spray, and brightness, and profound calm. With utmost caution, Jennifer disentangled herself from Ronald's arms and met his eyes in fear and wonder. They both peeked over the edge at once.

What Jennifer saw, she vowed to herself she would never forget. Far below them was spread a more beautiful valley than Jennifer had ever imagined. The river looped and meandered through meadows grown white and rust with autumn. Here and there groves of cedar and hemlock stood, the shade and repose of Elysian fields, of wilderness open and at rest. Containing the valley were walls of granite, pearl and gray. They rose tall and sheer and unbroken, smoothed by the brilliance of evening light.

She was so taken by this grand place, so willing to waste her time in it, that for a moment she hardly noted the improbable possibility of their rather airy vantage point. The boat had left the rapid behind and was falling, slowly, light as a leaf, down the face of the highest fall she had ever seen. And she could not see this one very well. The top was already indistinct, materializing out of sky, and the bottom was still so far below she could not yet hear the thunder of it. They were caught, somehow, safe in the middle, the boat resting fully upright and drifting down the face of the fall as if held by the strands of a parachute.

But there was no chute, and truth to tell, Ronald was much more disturbed by this than Jennifer could be, feeling as she did that the universe in its very nature had to be stocked with great surprises to be what it was. They both, however, peered over the side to see what might be holding them. Ronald said later that he thought he saw something like a giant swan, white as the spray of the waterfall and bearing the boat upon its back. But he couldn't be sure—the light of the sun was full in his eyes, and the spray all around them was more than dazzling, like a whole forest of chandeliers all dancing and exchanging places.

Jennifer later said it was not anything like a swan at all. What she saw was a woman reclining outstretched on her back, supporting the boat with clean white arms. The skin of the woman was pure as the stars, and her eyes were green as the dogwood in spring, green like the eyes of Lady Demaris—and like the eyes of the woman in her dream who had told her to find the goddess within. For a moment, she thought, the woman looked at her calmly and smiled. Her hair floated round her, bound at the brows by a circlet of flowers. It was blonde, and full, and the face that it framed held more contentment than Jennifer had ever thought possible. Whatever those green eyes saw in the world, Jennifer wanted to see for herself.

She looked much longer than she had intended, for suddenly the woman vanished in a rush of white, and the boat was bobbing in the echo and foam of a giant plunge pool among the rocks, and the waterfall stood like a curtain behind them, erasing the world of miracle.

Her eyes found Ronald's once again. She had never noticed how green they were.

12

THAT NIGHT THEY CAMPED by a cedar grove on the edge of a meadow, almost surrounded by a wide and glassy loop of river. When they had drawn the boat up onto the grass, the top of the waterfall high above shone rosy and golden in last light, and the sound of it was a pleasant pulse, as constant and quiet as the beating of their hearts.

They spoke sparingly as they sat on their blankets next to the fire that Ronald had made. The sky had cleared, and the stars were coming one by one, and too much talk would only retard their shy appearing—or so felt Jennifer. She was drowsy and dry before the fire, filled again with Chambers' wonderful soup and bread. Her flesh and bones felt the memory of churning water as one might feel the aftermath of a good massage. She lay her head on Ronald's shoulder, interested more than anything in a night of rest. The sky grew dark, and the full moon bloomed like an open rose at the top of the fall, silvering the meadow about them and making the stone cliffs pale and perfect, filling the gorge with a lake of light.

On the edge of sleep, Jennifer murmured the words that seemed to fit the occasion:

> *"Earth has not anything to show more fair:*
> *Dull would he be of soul who could pass by*
> *A sight so touching in its majesty:*
> *This Valley now doth like a garment wear*
> *The beauty of the evening; silent, bare—"*

"If it's wearing a garment," Ronald interrupted matter-of-factly, "then how can it be bare?"

"Ronald!" She looked at him sharply, then let her eyes rove the lovely contours of cliff in the moonlight.

He followed her gaze. "Well," he said, breaking the silence, "whatever a person's preference might be, you have to admit it's a perfect place for a reservoir. Pipe it south and they'll never have to care about drought again. The wilderness shall become a pool of water—that's how Dad would have said it anyway."

Jennifer drew back, now rudely and fully awake. "The dam?" she said. "Here?"

"Not here exactly. Perhaps downstream where the canyon narrows. But the enclosure is so symmetrical that I imagine the water will rise almost to the top of the waterfall."

"But here?"

"Jen, it just goes down to the ocean otherwise. Use it or lose it. And they *need* the water, after all."

She drew herself up. "*They* again. *They need.* O reason not the need," she hissed. "Gwen told me all about it."

"What's there to tell? It's no secret or anything." Ronald was whining.

"What's there to tell? What's there to tell?" She looked all about them and held out her arms in best stage style:

> "For this, for every thing, we are out of tune;
> It moves us not—Great God! I'd rather be
> A Pagan suckled in a creed outworn."

"A what?" he asked.

"And not 'Great God' neither, but the great earth goddess, mother of us all. You wouldn't understand, and you've never understood. You'd dam the stars with your precious theodolite if you could, and drain their light for some dark use of the distant future. And why? Why? Tell me, Mr. Science. I'm dying to know."

A long silence followed, but finally Ronald took the dare, reverting in his hesitant voice to the song he thought might calm her spirits:

> *"Tell me why the stars do shine*
> *Tell me why the ivy twines*
> *Tell me why the sky's so blue*
> *And I will tell you why I love you."*

Jennifer smiled in spite of herself, and surprised him by joining in the reply, a verse she had composed for him in a lighter moment:

> *"Nuclear fusion makes the stars to shine*
> *Photosynthesis makes the ivy twine*
> *Solar refraction makes the sky so blue*
> *And hormone secretion is why I love you."*

Their two voices lit up the sky, and he put his arm around her when they came to the end.

To Ronald's dismay, she promptly removed it and told him straight,

> *"Nay, good Lysander. For my sake, my dear,*
> *Lie further off yet; do not lie so near."*

And he did.

Jennifer remained by the fire, conscious of Ronald curled up in the shadow of the wood behind her, and conscious of her verbal cruelty. All for the sake of a larger and better cause than romance. He would have to learn.

She wrapped herself in her two wool blankets (Ronald had one, but she had William's in addition) and lay by the fire, watching it fade as the sparks flew upward and coursed the night like rising stars. Then she was no longer watching the fire, but merely feeling its warmth on her face. And soon she dissolved into embers of sleep.

Jennifer had hardly left her waking self when she saw she was back on a twisting path among tall hedges. Once again she found her way to the center of the maze and saw once more the striking woman with long dark hair, piercing her with emerald eyes. Between them the rose grew showy and red, reflected in the fountain beneath it and filling the air with rich fragrance.

"Pluck and find," the woman urged. There was a deep-throated elegance to her voice. "Pluck and find the goddess within."

But I tried that, Jennifer wanted to say. She could not get the words out.

As if to tutor her in the method, the woman reached and crushed the flower in her hand, then scattered the petals in Jennifer's hair and suddenly caught her about the waist. *Caught her up* was more like it, for Jennifer found herself rising quickly into the air with the arms of the woman tight about her. The day was gone and there were stars, and when she looked down she did not see the shrubs and flowers of a formal garden but the moonlit floor of Amoenas Gorge. Directly beneath her she saw herself sleeping, a homely dishrag of a girl, sprawled in her blankets beside the fire. She felt a sudden superiority, an elevation, the surprising knowledge that she could at will transcend herself and no longer succumb to the thoughtless oppression of professors in fact and professors in training. Fathers and fiancés alike could never know her hidden life, her inner richness, her secret vantage point within from which she could grace them from time to time with bittersweet drops of condescension.

As she thought these things her sleeping figure grew

smaller and smaller, and Jennifer felt the woman's arms slip
slowly away until she was merely touching her hand, mount-
ing the sky with the sureness of her own new power. Far from
being alarmed, she exulted, watching the moonlit walls slip by
in the night that glowed for her alone and not for sleepers.
Soon they cleared the top of the gorge, and she saw in a breath
the loom and shine of all Three Queens—South, Center, and
North—startling and soft like a heaving sea that bares itself to
the moon. And still they climbed, swirling now in a cold clear
breeze that came and went in delicious rhythm,

> *The winds that will be howling at all hours,*
> *And are up-gathered now like sleeping flowers.*

The woman took her higher yet, past the craters and crags
at the top of the Queens, till they seemed almost among the
stars, and she gestured with her hand that was not touching
Jennifer's, sweeping over all that was below them and all that
was around them, as if to say, "This too is yours, if you now
possess it. All earth and sky and the stars besides—these are
your footstool. Pluck and find the goddess within."

"Yes," said Jennifer. "Yes. Yes!" And she removed her hand
from the touch of the woman as if to claim her own.

In that very instant she began to fall. Not a gentle descent,
as she had known in the arms of the other strong woman with
the same green eyes, not the drifting down the face of the fall,
but a stark plunge, an accelerating drop that lifted her stomach
into her throat and kept it there, each moment worse than the
last.

She looked for the woman but could not see her. The stars
fell away, the shining bulk of the Queens rushed past, the forest resurged to the rim of the gorge, and the gorge itself
opened to meet her in terrible alacrity. There below by the
river their fire appeared, and the sleeping form of her lonely

self, and she wondered if she would fall on top of her, and which one would be crushed by the impact. The self became larger, and next to the head of the sleeping girl she suddenly saw the shape of a marmot, a very large one, crouched at her side and speaking obscenities into her ear. How she knew this from such a height she wasn't sure, but she supposed she was in both places at once, and so could listen.

The marmot and girl were coming up fast. She tried to scream—to warn *her* anyway if not *him* (for such a creature had to be male)—but no sound came. Instead she heard Ronald shout something confused like, "Hey! You! Hey! Beat it!" He ran up from the river swinging his oar, and the marmot fled, and Jennifer blessed him from barely on high. Then the ground and the campfire rose in a rush, and before she could even properly cringe she quite literally came to herself, lying quietly by the fire and watching Ronald stand panting above her.

All that moved was the trembling oar, held high in his hands against the stars.

13

"SO HE REALLY WAS THERE?" Jennifer asked it not quite as a question. The sun was high, and she and Ronald were drifting down the quiet river, watching the pearl gray cliffs slide past. Jennifer was at the oars, facing Ronald for comfort and letting him direct their course when the need arose. She was not bothering to row very often, and Ronald sat languidly erect in the stern, alert and at ease, trailing one loose hand in the water and holding the other under his chin. Their boots were off, and the wood of the boat was warm beneath their toes in the open but cool and mysterious under the arms of alder and cedar. The water was clearer here in the canyon—glacial milk become glacial wine—and here and there swam muscled salmon, sleek and red like the leaves of autumn, carving their way upstream from the sea to spawn at the foot of the great falls.

All morning long Jennifer had been on the verge of telling Ronald about her dream—about all her dreams. But she had held back, perhaps because a dream loses so much of itself when put into words; and out of pride, or privacy, or even the spell of the dreams themselves, she wanted to keep them only hers. Some part of her reflected, though, on how little they shared if she refused to share her dreams with him. These visions were like burdens to be borne—or when she thought of the dryad, like a mystery to be proclaimed. They startled and scared her, and Ronald might share their pain—though she knew what he'd do.

Not laugh, exactly. Ronald never laughed at such things. He would merely look down and lapse into silence, abstaining from any reassurance of voice or vote. She needed talk, and if not about the things that mattered, then about those that nearly did. And when she thought about it, the marmot mattered as much as her dreams, seeing it was in them—and out of them too—both at once, just as she had been in the night. So she asked about him one more time.

"It was there," said Ronald, "until it left. That is, till I chased it off. Though I wish I had gotten one good crack. I'd like to have flattened the thing with my oar. I could have, too." He lifted his fingers away from the lips of a curious salmon. "I mean, what was he doing? Eating your ear? Did you feel his teeth? Good thing I was up, checking the boat. I didn't want him tampering with *that*, not like last time, and then I saw him tampering with *you*. I wouldn't have looked, but you shouted something—I could hear you from down by the river. It sounded something like 'Less! Less!' Were you dreaming in your sleep? Do you remember saying anything like that?"

She shrugged her shoulders.

"Well," he said, "with a marmot like that sitting next to your ear, you're bound to have a nightmare or two. But he's gone for now." He paused to think out his next words. "In the future, I think, it will be my duty to sleep closer by." And he spoke it as if it were indeed his solemn duty. Jennifer felt charmed and amused and even grateful, all at once.

Just at noon they passed a fall on the northern rim, a free-floating ribbon that trailed from the snows of the South Queen, for here the river wrapped itself around the peaks on its doubled way to the Western Sea. Soon afterwards they pulled out onto a pleasant lea to eat the remainder of Chambers' bread. Jennifer found some wild onions, and so they had sandwiches after a fashion, and when they were done they took separate ways to bathe themselves in the heat of the day.

Ronald went upstream, barefoot in the dry grass, until he reached the creek that rushed from the base of the fall. Their own waterfall—the one they had so preternaturally descended —was now lost to view in these lower windings of the canyon. Each turn had brought new lawns, new groves, new stunning prospects of granite prows and shields and awnings mellow with the light of autumn. He was beginning to think that all of this might not look so fine when underwater. But he doubted he'd ever tell Jennifer that.

For a while he sat beneath the cedars that grew hard by and watched the stream purl over the mossy roots and mingle its life with the life of the river. It was a large creek, large enough for a few of the salmon that thronged the river to leap their way up it in quest of an end and a beginning. In the creek and in the river they flowed like blood against the current. *The water and the blood*, his father would say. He thought of William's terrible wounds at the very source, the staining of meltwater in the crevasse, and how fragile a rope was—how fragile a life—how easily cut by steel and ice. He thought of the blood that had steeped his hands, and the purifying ache of the stream, of the body borne in the bottom of the boat, and the losing of it. His father's voice returned again:

> They have taken the Lord out of the tomb, and we do not know where they have laid him.

And then he thought, as he always did without knowing it, of Jennifer, and why he loved her, a question incapable of solution. He remembered their going out into the hail in a thunderstorm, long ago on their You-Can-Do-It Expedition. They were looking for someone—a man who had fainted—but he remembered they'd found a rainbow instead at the end of the hail, and wet grass about their knees. He remembered how good and new it had felt to be with her, even though he hadn't known the words to say. Then as now, she was as cruel as she was kind, not losing the chance to embarrass him in his speechlessness. He told himself he did not mind, but wondered now if perhaps he did, and entertained for a brief moment the possibility of his protest.

In the midst of these considerations, he heard a sudden *bzeet! bzeet!* and saw the dark brown shape of an ouzel skimming down the creek through the trees. It came to a bobbing rest on a stone and looked him quickly up and down.

"Hello," said Ronald placidly. "You again." He wondered if it were another ouzel, but decided to believe it was not. The bird flew away back up the stream through the tunnel of trees. It paused for a moment amidst a small rapid, looked back, and flew further upstream and was gone from sight.

Out of curiosity and habit, Ronald followed, clambering over roots and logs and finding in places a path on the very edge of the creek. Before very long—for the floor of the gorge was rather narrow—he reached a misty amphitheater deep in a cleft of the granite wall and stood on the brink of a foaming pool, all turquoise and green, stirred by the touch of a feathery fall that might as well have dropped from the sky for all that Ronald could see of its top high above on the rim of the gorge. The amphitheater was tufted green with spray-laden moss and nodding ferns, and the white of the water was rich against it. The beat of the fall was strangely muted, and by the way that the ouzel, which he now saw, was flitting about and even through it, Ronald saw that the curtain of water was thin enough that he might have hopes of swimming out to it safely enough and combining his bath with a pleasant shower.

He was just about to remove his clothes and enter the water when he saw that someone had beat him to it. From behind a boulder far to his right an unclad figure suddenly dove into the pool and struck out with a whoop of delight for the fall itself. Once there, the figure sank in the foam and turmoil of water for quite some time—so long that Ronald began to fear he had witnessed a drowning. But then the person popped up with a shaking of hair and more whoops and shouts and swam splashing back to the waterfall to resubmerge himself again. *Himself*, for by the sound of the voice, Ronald was sure it was a man. Even so, he still felt like a peeping intruder, and decided to descend from the pool until the swimmer had finished his frolic.

He turned and left, unseen he hoped, and after a wait of perhaps ten minutes reascended to his vantage point beside the pool. The swimmer was gone. Not knowing quite what else to do, he cautiously approached the boulder from which the person had first emerged. Partway there, he noticed above him a trail winding improbably down a series of ledges on one side of the amphitheater, a trail which reached the bottom of the cliff just on the other side of the rock. He was about to step around the rock when he heard a voice, a young man's voice, speaking not to him exactly but not entirely to itself. He could not make out what the voice was saying above the noise of the waterfall, and then it paused, and Ronald was sure that the speaker had heard him, so he came a step closer to reveal himself and get the suspense over with.

But before the man came into view the voice began once again, and Ronald stopped, and this time he heard what it said:

> *"Your heart is made a waterfall, and I*
> *Would gladly slip away across the brink*
> *To plunge the waiting pool amidst the sigh*
> *Of green bright bubbles rising as I sink*
> *Down to a floor with granite pebbles lined,*
> *Each shining gently in a wat'ry light.*
> *Deep currents soft as willows will I find*

That silent swirl me round and lift my sight
Unto a canopy of spreading foam
Far tingling overhead in brilliant shade.
So quietly I float una wafting roam,
Till slowly toward the surface wreaths I fade:
But there you meet me in a lacy roar,
And plunge me to your green bright depths once more."

Though Ronald had heard a great number of poems from Jennifer's lips, it can be truthfully said that this was really the first poem he had ever *listened* to in his life. It excited in him a longing he could not begin to understand, and he stood with his hand on the moss of the rock with his legs all atremble, anxious to meet the man who spoke and to know the world as he knew it, but also anxious to hear more from his place of hiding. Caught between these two impulses, Ronald leaned closer so as not to lose a further word. Unfortunately, he leaned too far and came stumbling and tripping out from the boulder in an awkward attempt to right himself, falling at last at the outstretched feet of a young man wearing loose brown knickers who looked as surprised as Ronald was embarrassed.

"What's here?" said the man with strange good humor. "A little eavesdropper. An appreciator of *fine* poetry. Well, what's your business? Speak up." The young man, bare-chested, was resting on his elbows. He spoke from behind a full blond beard.

"I—I was just going swimming," Ronald said. "That's all. But I decided to wait my turn. And then I heard you, and wanted to listen. I thought you would stop if you knew I was here."

"Hah! Not likely," the young man laughed. "That I would ever stop, I mean. Though I did stop here at the foot of the trail, and as for the swim, I do recommend it. But how came you here, strange one? You're a long ways from El Ai, though I hear that some of your sort are in these parts nowadays."

"El Ai?" said Ronald. "You mean down south? No, I mean, I live near here, at least for the summer. Chambers Lake."

The man raised a thick blond eyebrow.

"But Jennifer and I, we came in a boat. We're going to the Tower of Otium, though we're not quite sure where it is. Do you perhaps?"

"And why might you be headed that way?"

"I don't know," Ronald confessed. "To be completely honest I have no rational idea."

The man relaxed. "Ah! Well, that's the best sort of trip. But who told you to go there—or that it *was* there?"

"A very old man," Ronald replied. "His name is Garth."

At the mention of this name, the young man suddenly rose to his feet. "And mine's Colin." He put out his hand as if in salute.

Ronald took it hesitantly. "Ronald," he said.

"I'm going to the Tower of Otium myself," Colin said. He crushed Ronald's one hand in both of his. "You're almost there. I'll show you the way."

Ronald felt grateful, as if he had been struggling for days with a task in the laboratory and Dr. Howe had suddenly appeared to competently put it to rights.

"But first," said Colin, "you really do need a swim."

The ouzel skimmed across the pool and came to rest on Colin's shoulder, bobbing in complete agreement.

14

As for Jennifer, when Ronald had left she stretched herself on the sandy shore of a quiet cove. She was on a bend of the river just downstream from where they had left their lunch and their boat. The cove was shaded by willow and alder rustling in a whisper of wind, but the sun shone warm on the sand where she lay, and she lingered there before undressing to bathe in the water. The unhurried quiet, the shy sublimity of the place, had a calming effect upon her spirit.

She looked over the water and past a grove to the rise of stone across the gorge and felt safe in its massive shelter. There was a rightness to its presence, and also to hers at the base of it; by being here she somehow undergirded its grandeur. She thought of the great gray flanks of granite as motherly in some distant way, something that could nurture her if she chose to let it, and something that she in turn could care for in age and time. And she thought again of her own mother, so calm in the midst of her father's perpetual agitation, and wondered if she felt her nurture even still.

She let her eyes drop back to the water and remembered the verse her mother had taught her that almost fit the present place:

> Dark brown is the river,
>   Golden is the sand.
> It flows along forever,
>   With trees on either hand.

Almost because the river, of course, was green, not brown—green as a lucent apple kiss unwrapped in her hand and almost placed upon her tongue. She begged her mother to buy that kind when they went to the store. But her mother was gone, and *ubi sunt*—where were the kisses of yesteryear? Dissolved in the surge and shine of the river. Somewhere, there, she longed for an answer, a glimpse that would make her less forlorn. And though she did not see Proteus coming, and failed to hear old Triton's horn, what she presently saw and heard was so strange and beautiful beyond her wildest hope or prayer that it suddenly seemed she might really see her mother again, on some very close and distant shore.

It caught her breath. What she saw came out of the river in the same inevitable way that Proteus was supposed to rise up out of the sea—except there was not one figure but dozens, as numerous as the burning salmon. For there in the cove the water was filled with the tender faces of strong young women. They emerged on a sudden, like riverine mermaids come up for air, their long hair spreading about their shoulders like lily pads in the green water. They looked perfectly human, and yet—well—too *wet* to be made of human flesh. Jennifer thought of the woman who had held their boat in the waterfall, and wondered if these were anything like her, and whether that woman might be here among them. The faces were half-turned from her; she quickly searched the pale wet profiles, but did not find the face she knew. Each one, however, held a restless beauty all its own, looking as if fully at ease to be in the river, yet eager to roam and course with the current, impatient to remain for long.

Their appearing took only the merest instant. For as Jennifer gathered these impressions, before she could even move or speak, the women in the water began to sing. First one poured out a single wordless quavering note, more like a flute than a human voice, and then another, in harmony, and yet another, adding to the diapason, until each joined each to create a chord so perfect and so various that the music of creation could not have been more pleasing to the ear.

And then there were words, a proclamation in unison that found its way into Jennifer's heart and promised to stay. The song was haunting, simple, edged with irresponsible joy:

> *"Sing ye trees and sing ye mountains*
> *Sing ye earth and sing ye sky*
> *Sing for mercy, sing for justice*
> *Sing for love that never dies.*
>
> *"Gentle sisters raise your voices*
> *Sing out clear and sing out high*
> *Sing for courage, sing for beauty*
> *Sing for love that never dies."*

The song was repeated, and then became antiphonal, echoing from one high wall and then the other. And then it renewed itself in a round, circling back on its end and beginning until all parts could be heard at once, until the song had no more first and last but was simply always, all at once. And then, suddenly, Jennifer realized the words had resolved themselves again to wordless notes, perfect meaning in pure sound, and she was not sure but that trees and mountains, sky and earth, had not joined the singers and answered the song by becoming part of it in that moment. She wanted to sing the words herself and include herself in the community of all that mattered. But something kept her, the same thing perhaps that finally kept her from sharing her dreams; and the notes ghosted away to an echo, and the beautiful faces, full of such purity and such longing, sank back in the water, each

> *like a creature native and indued*
> *Unto that element.*

And Jennifer kept silence, grateful for what she had seen and heard and nursing regret that she alone of all creation had failed to participate.

"Yes," said a voice, "the afternoon prayers are often the best."

Jennifer quickly swung about and half sat up. Standing behind her was a short blonde woman, pert and lively, and not much older than Jennifer herself. She wore a clean white blouse with an apron over a dusky skirt and like Jennifer was barefoot, except somehow magnificently so, as if shoes were things she never touched on principle.

"I come here each day just this time; at morning and evening they come to me in the cove at the tower. Perhaps you would like to hear them there—and sing, too, when you're given the courage?" Her face held a modest trace of humor, as if someday Jennifer might catch on.

"But who are they? And who are you?" asked Jennifer. She rather liked the woman already, but it seemed to her the invitation was a bit familiar, coming as it did from a stranger.

"To make the last first I am Rosamond," the woman said with an impish smile. "And these, of course, are the naiads—the ones, at least, who live here in Amoenas Gorge."

And so they might be, Jennifer thought. Naiads to wet the ancient lips of the dryad of her dreams. Ovid again. And yet, she sensed, something more and greater than Ovid.

"This was to be my last day to hear them alone. Though as it turns out, I have heard them with you, my sister. And gladly too—I think it is better that way—to prepare myself for companionship, for the sharing of joys. You are welcome here, and I must know you." Rosamond extended a hand.

"I'm Jennifer," said Jennifer shyly. She felt meek as she touched the woman's fingers.

"You marvel at me," Rosamond said, and she laughed like the ripple of the Amoenas. "Please do not. You have the pleasure of coming here on the evening of my wedding day. My attendants are poor and few. In fact, you have seen them all in the water. Not poor in spirit, for they see their Creator as we but hope to. But I was so much wishing for someone to come to be my bridesmaid. And see, Jennifer, you have been sent."

"Sent?"

"Sent by the Love that died and never dies, the Love that I shall become a part of in one small way, that always yearns to be part of us."

"Well, I *was* sent, though I suppose it was my fault that he had to send me—Garth, I mean. The old man. He was the one who told us to come."

"And Garth shall be here," she interjected, "at noon tomorrow, to perform the ceremony."

Somehow Jennifer wasn't surprised. They were all in cahoots, this community that stood for and within the wilderness. And she was relieved to know that Garth was coming. Maybe he would know what to do, how they might rescue the sleeping William.

But surprised or not, she wanted to know how Rosamond knew the strange old man. She was about to ask when Rosamond, looking up the shore, gave a start, and blushed, and opened her mouth but said nothing at all.

Jennifer got up off the sand and saw coming toward them a blond-bearded man who was running his course with evident joy. He was young and handsome, his shoulders draped with a roughspun shirt that could not hide the strength beneath it. Behind him, walking at some shy distance, was her own Ronald, glasses off and hair plastered wet to his scalp. The young bearded man came sprinting up and with scarcely a glance at Jennifer took the speechless Rosamond firmly and fully into his arms. For a moment, as she watched them kiss, Jennifer felt a twinge of jealousy—Ronald had never arrived like this.

But then Ronald did arrive, and quietly took her hand in his, and Jennifer found new hope in the present. The two of them stood patiently by the embracing couple without feeling any of the embarrassment they supposed they should. The love they saw was the love they might share.

"They're getting married," Jennifer whispered.

"I know," said Ronald. He seemed as proud of the fact as she did.

Then they were all four introducing each other, and all at once, so that Rosamond made them start all over until their names were justly distributed.

"Well then," said Colin at last, "if I've heard correctly, we're all headed for Otium?"

"Of course," said Rosamond. "Colin to come live with me and be my love, and Ronald and Jennifer to be each other's and our own." She swept her arms along the shore, inviting them to follow her down a faint path in the sunburnt grass. "There are many rooms in my father's house."

"No need to walk," Ronald said. "We have a boat that will carry two—and two besides."

"Then both may go!" Colin fairly shouted, and began to sing, laughing Ronald into confusion.

Rosamond readily consented to the plan, the more so when they all noticed a mass of thunderheads rising above the gorge downstream in the deepening heat of the afternoon. "If we put ourselves to it, we may yet prevent the storm," she said.

"But you can't prevent a storm," said Ronald.

"She means we'll get there first," whispered Jennifer, digging her thumbnail into his palm.

They quickly sauntered back to the boat, and before they got there the pile of cloud had shrouded and stolen the warmth of the sun. Colin took the oars by common consent, and Ronald and Jennifer squeezed together in the stern while Rosamond sat half turned in the bow, a much more pleasing ornament than the plain gray ouzel had been thus far. Speaking of which, it was no surprise to Jennifer that the ouzel itself came skimming downstream as they launched off, coming to rest in Rosamond's extended hand.

Colin rowed with sure strong strokes, pushing them ahead of the current at cunning and delightful speed. The borders of alder, of willow, of dogwood now, slipped by with the cedars on either hand, giving way to new meadow vistas of rock walls purple with thickening light. Deer lifted their heads from the grass and watched them go, sniffing the air of coming storm.

On the boat, the four of them held their tongues in quiet, all reverential, filled with the joy of expected surprise. What little breeze had been had ceased, and the only sound was the dip and plunge and creak of the oars, and the scattering of drops from the gleaming resurrected blades. The sky darkened, and darkened, and around a bend the wind returned, this time in erratic puffs, disturbing the surface of the river first here, then there, in gentle gusts.

Jennifer quickly dug their parkas from the pack at her feet. Colin, straining gloriously, said no when she offered one, so she passed it up to Rosamond and wrapped the other about both Ronald and herself. She felt wonderfully cozy, the way she once had years ago sitting next to him under a slick green fly they had failed to erect in a hailstorm. The fly had enclosed them side by side in the warmth of wool and huddling bodies. She looked at him now and wondered if he remembered that moment, if his mind associated that time with this.

She caught his eyes as if to ask, and thunder crashed like the noise and collapse of exfoliating sheets of granite. The wind gathered strength and direction, blowing upriver into their faces, and soon the air held drops of rain, falling at first like scattered pebbles. Then the sky shot aching white, and the thunder exploded in full strength, reverberating across the gorge and within their minds.

Colin swept them round a bend, and there before them, lit up in a mask of light, a huge stone pinnacle rose up out of the midst of the river. Jennifer got just a glimpse before the rain came down in earnest. The skirts of the rock were forested with benches of lawn, and facing upstream on the topmost bench was a generous cottage built into the side of the tower. Above the cottage the rock rose smooth and sheer and gray, narrowing to a tiny summit as high, it seemed, as the walls of the gorge on either side.

Jennifer took in just this much before sheets of rain filled the sky. The wind soon gave them a thorough perpendicular drenching, and she felt the water begin to collect in the bottom of the boat. She peeked at Colin, who was pushing the bow through windstung whitecaps, and saw that he wore a smile of pleasure. He winked at her and shouted heartily, "Perhaps you could use that bucket of yours?" Before she could move, Ronald found it under their seat and began to bail with a will.

The thunder now came without interruption. In a separate moment of sky-forked brightness, Jennifer saw through the pelting rain that they had almost reached the tip of the island. Instead of landing them there, however, Colin pulled the boat to the right, and she watched the island begin to slip by with the sudden worry that perhaps this was not the Tower of Otium after all—or, worse, that Colin and Rosamond meant to take them somewhere else, that they were not the friends they seemed. She looked at them with new sad eyes and put her hand on Ronald's knee.

Then all at once the rain was shut out, and Jennifer saw they were passing under a low stone bridge, a natural arch, that connected the island to the shore. The storm was suddenly distant and hollow, more echo than force.

When they floated back into the rain again it seemed less insistent, and Jennifer could see ahead down a long steep valley more like a V than the U-shaped canyon behind the arch.

At the end of the valley, where it turned beneath a generous flank of virgin forest, sunlight shone, the end of storm, and beyond it she saw ridge after ridge of soft dark fir that reached, perhaps, to the shore of the sea.

They had drifted almost past the island, and Jennifer really was beginning to worry about just where they were going, when Colin tucked them behind a sandbar and into an eddy with a few smart strokes, and then rowed the boat sedately back to a sandy cove at the foot of the tower. The rain stopped as they ran aground beneath the arms of a giant alder, and the thunder grumbled at half strength, retreating reluctantly somewhere farther up the canyon.

"Welcome!" said Rosamond, leaping from the bow. She helped Ronald with one hand and assisted Jennifer with the other, and they stood on the sand without letting go, the three of them laughing because they were so indescribably wet, though Jennifer thought perhaps that wasn't quite the reason. It was more the laughter of climbing partners on a snowy summit, of old friends at the front door, of children allowed an extra hour of freedom and play on a summer evening.

Colin hauled the boat ashore, and then joined their hands in a perfect circle. The westering sun broke under the clouds and illuminated his wet blond beard, and the tower behind them glistened like silver in rainslick polish. The ouzel reappeared in their midst, *bzee*ting and bobbing. Across the cove and down the valley a rainbow shone in the new-washed sky, resting its promise in rivers and mountains without end.

15

"YOUR FATHER'S HOUSE did you say this was?" Jennifer was sitting back from the modest table that was scattered over with empty plates, once again looking about the main room of the cottage. The shutters of the generous windows were opened upon a grassy terrace that dropped away through arbors and groves to the placid river that stretched upstream between the walls of the lower gorge, tinted with rose in the gentle dusk.

This was precisely the stretch of water they had navigated in sheets of rain through which she had gotten her first glimpse of the Tower of Otium. After landing in the cove behind the tower, they had circled back on a path that climbed through yellowing dogwood to wet lawny benches, each affording pleasant prospects that begged a day, a summer, a year, a life of slow contented contemplation. Then they had rounded an outcrop and found themselves before the cottage, built against the base of the tower and in this season amber—not green—to the very door. A spring bubbled out of the grass by the step and rushed away in a clear-flowing stream across the meadow and down to the river. It made Jennifer think of the fountain beneath the rose in her dream, and made the cottage more strangely precious in her mind.

And so Rosamond had lifted the latch and welcomed them into this common room, low-roofed with beams. There was a fireplace where Rosamond cooked at one end, the table at which they now sat in the middle, and another fireplace ringed with cushions on which they might recline at the other. Rosamond had taken Jennifer into a bedroom and helped her select a dry smock to wear, green like the river, and Colin must have found clothes for Ronald, for by the time Jennifer re-emerged both fires were lit and the two young men were standing about in gray knickers and clean white shirts. Then had come soup and warm buttered bread, and crumbs and laughter, and the scooting back of chairs in contentment.

"Indeed," said Rosamond. "My late loved father the Lord Amoenas, brother to the renowned Lord Linton of the western meadows, built this cottage for my mother after meeting and marrying her by the great falls at the head of the gorge. Here I was born, and here I grew in the care of my father after my mother burst smilingly in the labor of bearing a mortal such as I."

"Your mother—?"

"Well, *dissolved* is more like it, released to her native element."

"You mean—?"

"Yes. My father was an earthborn man, but my mother was the most beautiful of the mountain naiads. Though I have more of my father in me, and am well content to live warm and dry in the cottage he built, I serve as protectress, if not companion, to my cousins."

"Naiads?" said Ronald. He sounded a good bit over his head.

Jennifer thought how she might explain, and realized she couldn't. "You know—water nymphs. The river when it sings."

Colin clapped Ronald on the back and said, "You'll catch on, lad. It's nothing too difficult."

"Why, yes," said Rosamond. "Lord Linton, my uncle, was married to an oread princess, and Colin himself is dryad on his father's side. Cedar, I think. Or was it—"

"Oak," said Colin. "He came from the chaparral in the south."

Jennifer looked at Ronald again:

> "There are more things in heaven and earth, Horatio,
> Than are dreamt of in your philosophy."

"Horatio?" said Ronald.

But Jennifer, with questions of her own for Rosamond, left Ronald in his peaceable confusion. "You say you serve as *protectress* for the naiads? Whatever for? Who wants to harm them?"

"No one at all for the life of my father, and for the lifetimes of my mother's mothers. But since he died, and his body was borne in the sacred barge to the Western Sea, a king has arisen far to the south—the great El Ai (may his name ever perish). His empire grows by the desert hills of a thirsty land. The great El Ai is dissatisfied with the music of the chaparral and the drought-stricken brooks which sound in the place he has chosen. He has lately heard of my sweet-voiced cousins and coveted them for his private pleasure. Ever since my father died El Ai has come with his bands of thieves by horse across the desert and into the gorge to seize and carry away my cousins to bitter captivity far in the stinking pools of his city. I can do very little. And so it has been that Garth has given his permission for Colin and I to marry at last. For many years—the years of the Lava Beast—Colin could not be spared from his post in the western meadows, where he kept watch over the hapless marmots. The Beast yet lives, but his claws are blunted, and Garth has consented to our union so that Colin might help to protect the Amoenas."

"It's not all as practical as that," said Colin. "Garth too is a man who knows what it is to yearn and to love." He laid his arm upon Rosamond's shoulders and looked at her as if to scold.

"Garth?" said Jennifer. It was hard to envision a tender side to the stern old man she had met in the cave.

"Of course," said Colin. "Everyone knows of his former longing for the Lady Lira. When they were young and she was innocent, no two lovers loved as they. Whole days they spent—I have it in truth from Rosamond's father (may he rest and rise)—at the foot of the falls at the head of the gorge, singing what the water sang, and joining their voice to the voice of the naiads. Whole days they rowed the river together in every season—the rush of spring when the meadows are flooded and dogwood blooms above the current, the green of summer when the grass is tall and thick with flies, the quiet of autumn when the flies are at rest and the stalks of grass are dry and rusted, the hush of winter when the walls are traced by fingers of snow on every ledge and the great falls hide in a shield of ice. Here at the tower she and Garth would end their journeys and scale to the very summit by daring and invisible ways. From the top they would laugh in the face of the sun and watch it set and rise again before they returned—no one knew how."

"But what happened?" said Jennifer. "Why aren't they together now?"

Colin started to answer but stopped, looking to see if Rosamond knew how to explain.

"It's a long story, and very short," Rosamond said. "On the morning of their wedding day in the western meadows, Lady Lira disappeared."

"Abducted?" said Ronald. "Kidnapped?"

"Everyone would like to think so," Rosamond said. "But she seems to have left by her own free will, and to have spent the rest of her wretched years in the service of the Lava Beast, preying for him on the hoary marmots roundabout, and praying to him—if half the stories about her be true—in her mansion within the obsidian cliffs.

"And Garth, brokenhearted, yielded his ax after many years to one William Arthur, his chosen heir, so that Lady Lira might be dispatched. Finally, he chose between his love and his land. The deed was done, and Lady Lira was delivered up to the jaws of the Lava Beast himself, after the ax had betrayed her into the crater lake of the North Queen."

"So that was the end of her?" said Jennifer.

"All of us certainly thought so," said Rosamond. "There was the marmot, of course, the one she called James, whom she had corrupted to her service. He ran away at the last moment—but now he has attached himself to the great El Ai (may his name ever perish)."

"A very big marmot?" Ronald asked.

"Yes," said Colin. "A whistle pig if you ever saw one."

"But lately," said Rosamond, resuming her story, "word has come of a curious statue set up in the barren courts of El Ai. It is the very likeness of Lady Lira, only now she is known and worshiped there as Lady *Lyra*. So even in death she seems to have gained an apotheosis. The great El Ai directs all his people to bow down before her. She is, he tells them, the only goddess—the goddess of earth."

Jennifer felt a twinge of dismay. "This Lady Lira—or Lyra," she corrected herself. "What does—or did—she look like?"

"I have not seen the statue," said Rosamond. "But in life her face was as beautiful as the faces of her sisters—the precious Stella, drowned with the stars at a tender age; and Lady Demaris, who yet lives among us (she is the one who brought up Colin from orphaned boyhood at their father's home in the meadows under the Center Queen). Like her sisters, Lady Lira has the greenest of eyes. But her hair is black, a presage, I suppose, of her soul. Lady Demaris has hair that is the richness of cedar, and Stella's is a golden fire like the planets at dawn."

"Is?" said Jennifer.

"Is," said Rosamond. "Stella did not so much drown as commit herself to the stars and the waters high atop the North Queen. And she is seen in other places as well. Wherever rivers flow free or lakes lie pure beneath the sky, Stella is there."

"Even," said Jennifer, "in a waterfall?"

"Oh, especially there," Rosamond smiled. "You have seen her then?"

"I believe I have. And Lady Demaris at Chambers' cabin."

"And James," said Ronald. "And Garth, and William, and maybe even his ice ax, except now it's an oar—one of the two we have in our boat."

"Marmots have mercy!" said Colin in wonder.

"And Lady Lira," said Jennifer in a miserable whisper. "I think I have seen her in my dreams." All of a sudden she began to cry. For days she had wanted to tell someone, and now she was telling three people at once. She cried till her cheeks were very wet and the front of her smock was smeared and stained. When at last she stopped sobbing, she noticed that Ronald's arm was around her. He looked confused.

"Perhaps you have much to tell us," said Rosamond. "Let's clear the dishes and sit by the fire. It will be so much more comfortable and will give you a chance to recover yourself."

"I'm sorry," said Jennifer, getting up and feeling foolish for crying in front of everyone. She felt she had failed them in some way.

"No need, no need," Colin said brusquely. "You've said the right thing."

He stoked the fire and they settled into the cushions beside it, Rosamond leaning on Colin's shoulder and Jennifer propped up awkwardly against Ronald's knees. How long did it take, she wondered, for two people to learn to be one?

Rosamond nodded to Ronald first. "Give us your waking

tale, Ronald, before Jennifer relates her dreams. One is as needful as the other."

Conscientiously Ronald reported the story of their journey, with precise attention to time and distance and event, and rather less to how he felt about any of it. He faltered, however, when he came to the part about severing the rope on the bergschrund lip, and Colin groaned.

"Alas, poor William. I knew him once—not well, but once. Who knows? He might have learned to sing."

And when Ronald told about William's abduction, Colin hurled a stick in the fire. "That murderous marmot—may he be drowned and swallowed forever in the odious cesspool of El Ai."

"Can we get him back?" Jennifer pleaded. "William, I mean?"

"Garth will know," Rosamond said. "He will be here tomorrow."

"Garth or no, I will not marry until we do!" cried Colin. He jumped to his feet. "It would be a shame for me to lie in my Rosamond's arms and that man remain a captive in deep danger and disrespect. By the North Queen and all that is sacred, I swear it now."

Rosamond looked at him quietly for a long time. Jennifer wondered if she were disappointed at the sudden prospect of postponing their wedding day. "It is well," she said softly. "You have said, Colin. It shall be so. Only, let us wait for Garth." She nodded to Ronald to continue his tale.

Ronald went on hesitantly, explaining the help the ouzel had given them coming down the river.

"So that's where he's been these few days," said Rosamond. "I had wondered at his absence. Truly you had a reliable guide."

When Ronald explained their descent of the falls they

expressed no surprise, though Colin admitted to feeling envious.

"Once in a lifetime a mortal may descend that fall," said Rosamond. "My father, Lord Amoenas, came down that way on the day he met my young sweet mother there at the bottom. It is a sign of a great commission—an honor and a great delight. You must cherish that day—it will nourish you in the steep dry years that lie ahead."

And then Ronald was finished, and Rosamond looked sorrowfully at Jennifer. For a moment Jennifer kept silence. But then she told, reluctantly at first, her dream in the tent of the maze and the rose and Lady Lira, and of the actual rose she had plucked from the ax (which was Stella's, said Rosamond), and the dream of the dryad beside the cedar, and of James the marmot gnawing at William, and of seeing Lady Demaris again, and finally—this took the most courage to tell—of her dream in the gorge of ascending the night sky high above the Three Queens and her sleeping self.

"So she lives," said Rosamond thoughtfully, "at least in the voice of her sometime marmot, speaking into your ear by night. It is strange, but one part of me is sorry for her yet. The three of them were such splendid sisters—and she suffered so in her cruelty. And now to have her depraved shadow seducing you in your dreams, Jennifer. It is altogether sad, both for you and for her memory.

"But rest assured, Jennifer, she is not your goddess within. With the naiads, know your Creator without and he will dwell richly within you. Lady Lira forsook and denied both him and his gifts, and her marmot would fain have had you believe we are self-created, each queens in our kingdoms, but the truth is something much humbler, and better. To serve and to worship in our small places is to be gifted with all creation, and to know the gift of our true selves."

"Amen to that," said Colin. "Except—I cannot confess such

tender feelings for our dear departed Lady Lira. I have a mind, in fact, should I find her statue, to hack it to chips with a good stout ax and feed them to the nearest fire. The old witch! You are too soft, Rosamond. She got exactly what she deserved, and I wish she had gotten it a good bit sooner than she did. Old James has a score to pay. I hope we get there before poor William is sacrificed to his live will and her dead pleasure. That's what I think. Sorry indeed!"

Rosamond sighed and exchanged a glance with Jennifer as if to say, with a certain melancholy, "Men!" But she chose not to reply.

By now the evening had grown late and the fire had begun to die. Ronald proposed that he and Colin sleep out by the cove to guard the boat from any harm, and leave the cottage to the women. Colin thought this a most sensible plan and set about gathering wool blankets to offset the wet chill that lingered in the air in the aftermath of the thunderstorm. Jennifer had half a mind to accompany them—it seemed rather odd to sleep indoors—but the thought of remaining with Rosamond was so comforting that she stayed with pleasure. So it was that they kissed their men good night at the door and watched them pace off into the moonlight to do their duty.

The two of them stood there in pleasant silence, looking out through the open doorway down the glistening lawns to the river. The air was cold on Jennifer's cheeks. She watched the glint and gleam of the water, the ghostly polish of canyon walls, and thought she heard the distant sound of silvery singing. She found she was clasping Rosamond's hand in the innocent way she used to stand with her mother or a childhood friend. "I like this place," she said to her softly, "and willingly could waste my time in it."

"Let's," said Rosamond, and led her back into the cottage.

She slept that night on a soft grass pallet in a separate room, dim and dry, closing her eyes amid the echo of naiad song that came in through an open window. It seemed she had scarcely fallen asleep when she dreamed again of the garden maze, the turnings of path among tall thorny hedges. She came as before to the center of the garden, the enclosure of hedge about rose and fountain and beautiful woman whom she now knew to be Lady Lira, in death as in life. The woman stood tall in her crimson gown and regarded Jennifer knowingly.

"Pluck and find," she said again, pointing to the rose in the hedge. "Pluck and find the goddess within."

"No," said Jennifer. She felt surprise at her resoluteness.

Without even seeming to hear her, the woman plucked the rose herself, this time with a strangely mechanical motion. Immediately the red rose wilted in her hand, turning brown, then black in a shrunken corpse of its fragrant self. The spring at her feet abruptly dried up. Most surprising of all, the woman herself began to age before Jennifer's eyes. Her clear fair brow contracted in wrinkles, her nose grew knotted with hairs and warts, and her emerald eyes became dark and deep-sunken. Her back stooped, her hands shook with the tremor of palsy, and her crimson gown hung tattered and gray.

"Pluck and find," the old woman rasped. "Pluck and find the goddess within."

Then in her dream a voice from behind Jennifer said, "Come out, dear sister. Oh please, come out. You may still come out from the belly of the Beast. There is yet time, and you are yet loved."

Jennifer turned to see standing behind her the woman she had seen in the waterfall, the woman Rosamond had called Stella. She stood young and fresh and golden-haired in a robe of white. What struck Jennifer was the pureness of pleading in her face, the longing that not one should be lost. Here, she thought, was sisterly affection as she had never guessed could exist.

The hag that once had been Lady Lira repeated her hollow invitation. "Pluck and find. Pluck and find the goddess within."

"Oh, sister!" cried Stella, and rushed past Jennifer to grasp Lady Lira by both hands. "Don't you see? I am here. You are given a chance to know the mercy from without."

Lady Lira paused a moment, as if dimly aware of a presence at the margin of self. "Pluck and find," she rattled out.

"Oh, sister," Stella repeated softly. She went down on her knees, still holding the hands of the hag, and began to weep. "My poor lost Lira."

What Lady Lira might have done, Jennifer was prevented from knowing. For in that moment a clatter awoke her; outside her window she heard the hooves of many horses. And before she could separate dream from waking, the door to her room flew open with a crash.

16

WHEN RONALD AWOKE, the morning was no longer young. There on the sand in the shade of the tower, lulled by the steady surge of the river, he had slept deliciously and long. Colin's blankets lay broken like an empty cocoon. Ronald found his glasses in a boot and put them on to look for Colin and find his world. The boat lay undisturbed nearby. The alder trees clumped next to the beach held out their leaves, sere and serene. Swallows swung across the cove, flash upon swirl, and arced high to their nests on the face of the tower above.

Ronald remembered what Colin had said about Garth and the young sweet Lady Lira climbing the tower to its top by daring and invisible ways. Invisible indeed. Now in the shadow of morning light the tower looked more than impossible to scale. Polished smooth by millennia of glacial ice, it raised its needled head at least a thousand feet above the river. Geologically, the spire was an anomaly. Only the very toughest granite could hope to withstand the midstream force of a valley glacier. Somehow the rock had remained what his father might have called, in the only poetry Ronald could remember him speaking,

> *an ever-fixed mark,*
> *Whose worth's unknown, although his height be taken.*

In the course of his fieldwork Ronald had climbed a few rock faces, but he could not imagine anyone wanting to venture out onto this one.

He was still reposing in his blankets, pondering the face of the tower with a strange mixture of scientific curiosity and metaphysical satisfaction, when he heard a howling in the distance, and soon saw Colin descending the trail to the cove at a run. It was Colin himself who howled as he went, and when he reached the sand he beat his breast and stumbled to Ronald in a disheveled frenzy. He stood shaking and panting for some moments, unable to speak, then closed his eyes and labored himself into a calm.

"What's the matter?" said Ronald, standing up in his blankets. "Tell me. Please." He shook Colin's shoulders, but couldn't get him to look in his eye.

At last Colin began to speak, with a slow sadness in his voice:

> "I saw her face in the aspen grove,
> Composed where the wind and branches wove
> A halo of dusk-burned clouds in her hair,
>   And she was fair.
>
> "I saw the night in her doe-brown eyes,
> Deepening in the clear moonrise,
> Her gaze abstracted and warm and cold,
>   And she was old.
>
> "I smelt the sage in the silver sky
> And heard the stream that was rushing by
> To sink in the desert sand like thought,
>   And she was nought."

"Not *what*?" cried Ronald. "*Who's* not? And what's all this about aspen and sagebrush? None of that here."

"Plenty of it where we're going, lad," Colin replied. He spat in disgust.

"Where we're going?"

"The dusty trail to El Ai, young one. Rosamond and Jennifer are halfway there, and not by their own free will, I can tell you. Sleep on the beach—of all the blundering ideas! Taken in the night, and probably the whole pack of naiads with them."

"You mean—"

"He means you have a long journey ahead." Ronald turned to see Garth, white-haired and white-bearded, standing beside them, his pace of coming unperceived. It seemed rather fitting for him to appear. Still, Ronald was quietly amazed.

"Journeys have a way of begetting journeys. You must accept each one that comes. And you as well, Colin. Young Ronald was not at all wrong to sleep in the sand beside the boat, and you must not regret keeping him company. The contents of this bark are precious, and your faithfulness, Ronald, shall be rewarded."

With that, Garth stepped to the rowboat and reached inside with both arms. What he brought out, one in each hand, were not oars but axes—the axes that the oars had been on the Center Queen. He held the shorter out to Ronald. "Take this ax, the ax of the rose, of the pure drowned stars. Let it work its grace on those it may touch. Let it know the hands of a woman."

Ronald received the ax with care, and nodded in bewilderment.

Colin reached for the longer ax, the one that was William's, but Garth withheld it. "This ax I will keep for myself, and I myself will keep here until you return, to use it as I am used by it. I thought I would never hold it again, but with it now in my hands I feel a rousing motion within me. As I see you here, ready for your journey, my old age knows the strength of its youth. Though much is taken, much abides. Go then, both of you, and return if you can to bear the body and to wed. You have my blessing and my hopes."

As Garth completed his benediction, the sun emerged from behind the tower and flashed upon the silver head of the short wood ax in Ronald's hands. He felt rather dazed. To wake and to lose and to leave in a moment was much at once. If only he could return to the glacier and simply finish his movement survey. To make the world into numbers in a data book—how much simpler that was than oars and axes capriciously interchanging themselves.

Instead of expressing this longing for a familiar world, Ronald allowed himself to be taken back up the path to the cottage. Halfway there, as they circled the tower, they passed a trail which led down and across the natural bridge to the shore of the river closest to the Three Queens. This path, Ronald imagined, must lead to the tall thin waterfall where he had met Colin, and thence up many a narrow ledge to the valley rim and the outermost skirts of the South Queen. When they reached the meadow in front of the cottage, Ronald saw that their path dipped down to yet another natural bridge that joined the tower to the opposite shore. Across this bridge, quite long and quite slender, a trail zigzagged up a ravine and disappeared at the southern rim. He didn't need Colin or Garth to tell him that this was the way they would be going.

The meadow itself was plowed by the hooves of many horses, clods of earth strewn everywhere atop trampled grass. The spring was muddied and manured, and the door of the cottage was wrenched askew, hanging halfway off its hinges. They walked inside, and the room which had brought such order and comfort the evening before now lay in shambles—the table collapsed, the cushions shredded, the ashes spread about the floor.

"And look here," said Colin, shaking his fist. He showed

them into the bedrooms in back. In each of them the empty
beds were deliberately cracked asunder, broken in two from
head to foot. Suddenly Ronald was roused to a fury he had
kept himself from feeling till now. He thought of Jennifer
pertly recording his data in the survey book, and then of the
marmot gnawing the pages, and all at once saw the violation—not of his numbers but of her fingers, the work of her
hands.

"Neither heights nor depths," vowed Colin firmly, "neither
river nor plain, shall separate me from the love of Rosamond.
What say you, Ronald?"

"Much the same," Ronald mumbled, "in regards to
Jennifer, of course."

Colin looked askance at Ronald.

"He is saying what he can, Colin," Garth interposed, "and
means as well and as deeply as you. Now, couple your words
with deeds, and go."

Colin nodded, and they re-entered the common room.
From the wreckage of the kitchen he gathered provisions for
their pockets and slung flasks of water across their chests. "No
packs," he said. "We're going light. Can you run, lad?"

Before Ronald could answer, Colin was out the door and
gone. "Well, good-bye," he said uncertainly to Garth.

Then he was off, sprinting down the trail to the bridge and
onto it just as Colin crossed to the other side. If he hadn't been
trying to catch up to Colin he would have slowed to a careful
walk—the stone arch was slender indeed, wide enough for a
mountain horse quite sure of its footing but not any wider. As
he raced across he dizzied himself with the perpendicular
surge of the river, flaming with salmon some ten or twenty feet
below.

Then he was over, and the trail plunged into a cedar grove
and began to follow a tiny stream away from the gorge. He
couldn't see Colin. The way steepened into the ravine that he

had noticed from the cottage, and the cedar gave way to hanging thickets of slide alder through which the trail began to switchback in quick short turns, crisscrossing the stream at every traverse. The path was so narrow, so barely cut into the tangle of trunks, that he would not have thought horses could come this way had there not been the hoofprints to prove it. He ran up and up the green-gold tunnel, and still no Colin. His thighs ached, and his lungs hurt, and the ax grew heavy in his hands, and finally Ronald could run no more. The air was close inside the ravine, and his shirt and knickers were drenched with sweat.

Perhaps as much as an hour later, after running and resting several times, Ronald found Colin impatiently waiting at the rim of the gorge on a mossy ledge. "Sorry," said Ronald, and planted his ax in pathetic exhaustion.

"That's what rowing a boat does for you," Colin huffed. "But rest your mind. That's the steepest it gets."

Ronald stood panting and looked back down at the river below them. He saw the ribbon of fall, just upstream on the other side, and the trace of a trail on the cliffs beside it. Behind the fall was the forested skirt of the South Queen, silvered in its autumn ice, and behind the South, the familiar summits of Center and North, arranged in a column so that he could not see the pass that held Chambers Lake and their one-time camp. About the Queens the forest spread in every direction, broken only by golden larches and amber meadows and the creamy gash of the gorge below.

And within the gorge, directly before them, was the tiny summit of the Tower of Otium, exactly even with their feet. It was flattened off at the very top, with a crack that separated two small pedestals, each no bigger than what a single person could stand on. With a very long rope one might construct a Tyrolean traverse from summit to rim. It seemed quite odd,

Ronald thought, to be looking at a spot so close at hand which he might never hope to visit.

Before Ronald had rested quite enough or drunk more than a sip from the flask at his chest, Colin sped off once again. From here, one trail branched left and followed the top of the canyon upstream. Ronald supposed that William had been brought that way. Their own trail continued up and away from the rim through open slopes of western hemlock, bearded with lichen and stolid in self-sacred shade. As Ronald gathered his nerve to continue, he thought of the ouzel he had followed through just such a hemlock forest to find the boat when it had escaped. He thought of the ouzel and unashamedly wished him back, and also wished for the finding now of more than a boat—of Jennifer, and of himself.

Newly resolved, he trotted on. The trail rose in gentler, longer switchbacks now, and Colin stayed one turn ahead, passing through the trees above him as if he were going somewhere different, on another errand than the one he and Ronald shared. He stayed one turn ahead, but no farther. This time Ronald kept Colin in sight, and this in itself kept him going in spite of a terrible stitch in his side. He balanced the shaft of the ax in his hand, moving it back and forth like a piston, and heard in his pain the lonely song of the varied thrush like a distant whistle urging him on.

After more switchbacks than anyone would care to count, the hemlock thinned to Douglas fir and sugar pine along rocky ravines that hid a few scant patches of snow left over from winter. The trail wandered through dust and talus, humble phlox and blazing larch, and finally crested a real divide at a small gray tarn in a shingled depression. Colin was looking blankly at the water when Ronald arrived, each panting as hard as the other. The sun was dissolved in high cirrus scud, and far past its prime.

"Well run, lad." Colin offered his arm. "You see where

we've come." Ronald looked down a nearly endless forest slope to a distant suggestion of the gorge and the hazy shape of the Three Queens.

"And you see where we go." He guided Ronald around the tarn and stood with him where the ridge fell away at the opposite end. The trail plunged down through rocky clefts to a barren desert far below. No ancient hemlock interposed their verdure here. Close at hand were whitebark pine and juniper, then ponderosa and golden glimpses of aspen and cottonwood, and at the base of the ridge, stubborn groves of live oak amid skirts of gray-green chaparral. Beyond this, the desert opened south and east, dun beneath a strange dun haze. At its far extremity hills arose, barely distinguishable from the air. And at the foot of these hills lay a small dim spot, hazier than any other place to be seen.

"Behold El Ai," Colin said simply.

"Why all the smoke?" Ronald asked. "What's there to burn?"

"Not much," said Colin. "But the great El Ai requires every inhabitant of his great city to constantly burn an offering to him. Nothing live is sacrificed—or so at least I have heard—except the chaparral and the few growing trees that are at hand. And farther and farther from hand they get. The plain before you was not always the completely barren desert you see—just as the river which drained its edge beside those hills did not formerly run dry. Each outlying citizen is also required to build a large reflecting pool beside his home—some, I have heard, are acres long. These are to mirror and multiply the glory of the great El Ai whenever he chances to walk by, just as the smoke is to fill the air with the precious incense of his presence."

"You have been there then?"

"Never. But El Ai was the home of my mother, whence she fled across the desert and found comfort in the shade of an oak at the foot of this ridge, the Dark Divide. In gratitude she gave herself to him, and I was born of mortal and dryad months later in the promised land of the Three Queens. My mother (may she rest and rise) told me all. I have never been to El Ai. I have always feared it would come to me, and now it has."

He sat down wearily, pulled a few broken biscuits from his pockets, and shared them with Ronald. As they ate, Ronald wondered what it would be like to have an oak tree for a father. He thought of his own, stern and inflexible, rooted in the wooden pulpit which he seemed to inhabit in Ronald's memory, world without end. In a way he too was descended from oak.

Colin pointed to the tarn at their feet, printed with the hooves of horses. "They might have been here at dawn," he said. "A place to rest and water the horses and tighten the saddles before plunging down the dry side and into the desert." He sank and sighed and looked back toward El Ai with lackluster eyes.

"So what are we waiting for?" Ronald said bravely. He stood up and refilled his flask in the tarn. And paused. For a moment he saw a face in the water that wasn't his own. It was the face of an old thin woman, weeping and moaning for her children. But the moaning was the wind, and the wind erased the face in the water. Ronald wondered if he had seen a naiad of sorts, and if he had, if it were one that had just been brought here or one that was native to this pool on the Dark Divide.

He wasn't even sure enough of what he had seen to report it to Colin. As they hurried down the trail at a run, jolting not panting around each switchback, Ronald kept the face in his mind, superimposed in a grotesque way upon the image of Jennifer. Though he was thus preoccupied, he took care not to turn his ankle, nor to slip on the carpets of needles that occasionally covered slabs of smooth black rock in the trail. Sometimes, in fact, he went out of his way to kick a pine cone

or two—even those from the sugar pine that lay big as marmots across the path.

This time Ronald led the way, gathering the strength that
Colin seemed to be losing as the day drew on. They descended
through groves of yellowing aspen in tall white meadows, feeling the tang of evening air. They passed cottonwoods beside
trickling streams and lost themselves lower down in head-high
tangles of manzanita, just as they'd squirmed through thick
slide alder coming up the ravine from the gorge. The ground
became red and dry and hard. As the sun set over their right
shoulders, the earth agreed with its garish light as its natural
color, only less fierce than the blood-soaked bark of the
manzanita.

Just at dusk, they stopped descending and entered a grove
of large live oak at the very edge of the desert plain. The day
of running had taken its toll, and they sat in the shade of a
gnarled giant whose limbs spread out and down all around
them, offering rest. Ronald felt a sense of expanse and shelter,
as if they had found an empty pavilion. It was peaceful and flat
here. The ground was hard, but they sat among stalks of white
wild oats spread out among the trees like snow. Here and there
a bright-limbed sycamore rose among the somber oaks.

Ronald had blisters on both feet and was going to tell Colin
when both of them heard something—voices, they thought—
at the desert end of the twilight grove.

"Did we catch them this soon?" Ronald whispered. He ner-
vously gripped the head of his ax.

"Hardly possible," Colin answered. "But stay here—I'll find
out."

Colin crept off before Ronald could object. As he waited,
night truly came. There was the chirring of crickets, the click-
ing of a bat, and the sounds of small unknown creatures that
slid and skittered about in the oats. When Colin returned, one

star had come out and the moon had just begun to rise. The light of a campfire was visible away through the trees.

"They're from El Ai, but they're coming, not going," Colin whispered. He sat hard by Ronald against the trunk of the spreading oak.

Laughter echoed from the fire, and Ronald wished that he could share it.

"A woodcutting expedition," said Colin—"more fuel for the sacred flames. They've completely denuded their own hills, so now they come this far. Four of them—and six horses. And a wagon, I think. They haven't chopped anything down yet—they are just arrived. But they'll turn in soon to rest themselves for their work tomorrow. And that, my friend, is when we borrow hooves for our feet and axes aplenty for our hands."

Ronald stiffened. "You don't mean—"

Colin shook his head. "No, of course not. I wouldn't murder the great El Ai himself in his sleep. We'll leave them here to enjoy the oaks intact at their leisure. By the time they wake we'll have crossed the desert and be waiting at the gates of the city. It will be quite simple."

Colin seemed to have regained his morning's eagerness. Ronald too, aching and footsore, smiled at the prospect of cantering over the desert by moonlight. He lifted his ice ax, curiously out of place in this spot, and tapped it against the oak with approval.

"It is a good plan, my son," came a solemn voice. "Only this—*we* shall go with you."

Ronald jumped up. He could not tell who it was that had spoken. Then he saw Colin slowly rise and embrace the trunk of the tree itself.

17

IN THAT SAME TWILIGHT, Jennifer reached the gates of El Ai in loathing and relief. She had sat the same horse since the middle of the previous night, a sweating roan that shied on the switchbacks and lurched on the slabs, and that crossed the desert at a dismal trot which jolted her up and down in the saddle until her bones cried out for mercy. The prospect of journey's end was pleasing of necessity. But the farther they rode from the Tower of Otium, the more alien the land became. As gorge and hemlock gave way to desert and sage, her heart sank. This world was not her home.

But at least she had a horse to herself. Each of the naiads was forcibly mounted between the arms of a swarthy horseman. They had struggled at first, singing in pain and trying to slip off the bows of the saddles, but when day had come they had wilted in the manzanita, and now in the desert they were all but dead, draped across the horses' necks like broken lilies.

Rosamond had the worst of it. The largest and burliest of all, the great El Ai, who had come himself on this expedition, had chosen her to share his saddle. He was rather big-bellied, with a pink scarf wrapping his bald head and a red silk shirt half opened on his chest. To Jennifer he looked all too much like the disagreeable Escee. As he rode with Rosamond he constantly bent his cheek to hers, calling her his "pretty piece of Otium." He tried to share his cakes with her when they stopped to breakfast beside the tarn on the Dark Divide. And the sort of attentions he wished to give her now that they were arrived at El Ai were all too clear. He had captured not only a choir for his court but an unwilling concubine for his bed.

But Jennifer had no idea what they wanted of her.

The men who opened the massive gate in the sandstone wall looked much like the ones on horseback beside her—not so much swarthy as carefully tanned, and for all their cruelty rather spiritless. For miles outside the city gates they had passed strange rambling houses in the desert, each with its own reflecting pool and roaring bonfire at the door. The inhabitants stood next to their pools as the cavalcade passed, not even looking up at the horses, but merely staring down at the water and repeating the words, loud enough so Jennifer could occasionally hear, "I love El Ai, I love El Ai." There was no real fervor in the way they said it, but no real sense that they had any other sentiment to express either. The men at the gate said the same thing. It was not only mantra, but apparently the sole means of communication. Jennifer's captors had talked and cursed and laughed and argued all the way over the Dark Divide, brandishing swords and battle axes in high spirits, but once they had got within sight of the city they had fallen silent, letting their weapons hang in their scabbards and only exchanging the reassurance that they, too, loved El Ai.

Outside the city were no flowing streams and no standing trees. A long low bridge before the gate crossed a riverbed that was dusty and dry, and for miles about there was scarce a bush. The setting sun did not bring the tang of autumn cold but merely an anemic chill, bland and barely noticeable. It no longer seemed like autumn at all, nor summer neither. In fact, in El Ai it did not seem to be any season in particular. Every season, Jennifer guessed, was merely and purely the season of smoke. Her eyes smarted in the pall from the fires.

The horses entered the city proper at a tired walk—only it was not a proper city at all. The homes outside the city walls were richly furnished in spite of their irregular design, but the homes on the inside were mere hovels, crumbling huts of weathered sandstone looped and windowed in ragged decay. Equally ragged families sat beside cooking fires in the open doorways. Their skin held a native darkness deeper than the cultivated tan of the men in the cavalcade. None looked up as the party passed; none vowed their attachment to this place or to its august person either. Jennifer wondered if the great El Ai, riding just ahead of her, was in any way miffed by this lack of customary attention. But he was too occupied in trying to nuzzle Rosamond, and did not particularly seem to care if anyone else loved him or not.

They wound through the darkening streets, past many more hovels and cooking fires, until they reached a sandstone palace raised in the very heart of the city. The front of it was all towers and arches silvered in the rising moon, the sort of place Jennifer might ordinarily take interest in for the quaintness of its architecture. As it was, she was much too angry and much too tired to appreciate its finer features. They entered a large gate into a courtyard, where troops of servants bearing torches relieved the horsemen of their mounts. The naiads were passed to waiting hands and carried up a gleaming stairway like so many empty sacks of horsefeed.

"James!" thundered the great El Ai, swinging himself and his prize from the saddle.

"What?" said a voice.

Jennifer could not see who had answered, but noted the voice was from somewhere very close to the ground.

"James!"

"What?"

"Open your flesh-clogged ears and listen! Lodge this brace of maids for the night. I would have them now, but I must sleep. I trust none other to keep them close. Bring them to me when morning comes—that one first." He pointed at Rosamond.

"But the sacrifice, great one," said the voice. Jennifer had got down off her horse and now saw that the voice came from something sitting up like a dog. And not like a dog either, but like a marmot—a very fat one.

"What about the sacrifice, beast?" said El Ai impatiently.

"It is set for dawn, at the waning of the full moon. Shall they attend you there?"

"Oh, very well," grumbled El Ai. He turned his back on the dutiful marmot and made a deep bow to Rosamond and Jennifer. "Tomorrow, my favored ones. Rest before pleasure." He made the pretense of a smile and then with the help of several servants heaved his bulk up another stairway, opposite the one up which the naiads had been taken away.

"In the temple then," the marmot called after him. "We shall await you."

Soon Rosamond and Jennifer were left alone in the courtyard under the smoke-smeared stars with James the marmot. He turned his baleful eyes upon them, and Jennifer recalled the times she had met him before—in camp, on glacier, by riverside. A dozen epithets rose in her mind—*pig! brute! rodent! murderer!*—but they stymied each other and she kept dull silence. When he nodded his head and dropped to all fours they followed him mechanically.

He took them through a small door between the stairways and down a flight of sandstone steps to a dank apartment lined with straw. There was no furniture, no windows. A single candle burned in a niche. The marmot stood up and blew it out, then left the room and shut and locked the heavy door. They heard him shuffle back up the steps.

"Pig!" shouted Jennifer. "Brute! Rodent! Murderer!" She sat down next to Rosamond.

"He's deaf," said Rosamond in the dark. "Besides, he would take those titles as a compliment."

"We're blind," said Jennifer. "And I mean much worse than I say."

Rosamond sighed.

"I can't believe it," Jennifer went on. "So that's why I had a horse to myself. You I can see—but he wants me too. The great El Ai is getting hard up."

"Yes," said Rosamond. "The business is altogether disgusting, I agree. But—" She paused. "But in one small sense, you insult Ronald by what you say. To give yourself to a husband, Jennifer, you must believe you have something to give."

Jennifer was surprised to be handed this reproach and hardly knew how to respond. "He was all over you!" she exclaimed. "How could you stand it?"

"It *was* trying," Rosamond said. "His breath was rather like rotting carcasses of salmon that wash up on shore this time of year. But my dear lost naiads . . . I think of their poor desiccated souls almost more than I think of you or me, Jennifer. I cannot be sure they have survived the journey."

"Do you think they will come? Ronald and Colin. And Garth perhaps?"

"They will try," said Rosamond firmly. "We must hope. And sleep."

There being no other or better choice, they lay down together, nestling close in the stale straw. Jennifer did not sleep at first, though her limbs were sore and tired with travel. Her thoughts made pilgrimage to Ronald, wheresoever he might be. She wondered that he loved her at all, and if he loved her enough to risk himself in pursuit of her here. Looking on darkness with open eyes, she imagined his face

a jewel hung in ghastly night

and even then no quiet found.

Her sleep was restless. The marmot stood on one side of

the river and Garth on the other, arms upraised in execration or benediction, she wasn't sure which. The great El Ai rode back and forth on the bridges of Otium, and a voice repeated, "No such roses see I in her lips." An ice ax swirled above the tower unhanded by anyone, and Stella kneeled by the cottage fountain with her hands outstretched, proffering a burning coal. "No," rasped a voice. "Pluck and find. I am a woman of unclean lips. No, no."

Which was precisely what Jennifer found herself saying when the door to their cell burst open. James stood implacably over them between two men with burning torches. "Yes," said James. "I say yes, and you must come. Think of it as your ceremony of dedication to the great El Ai. The time has come, and you are in it."

They rose reluctantly, stiff and sore, and followed the marmot back up the steps to the courtyard. The air was cool and pale and smoky in first light. He took them up the stairway that the naiads had been carried up the night before. Then he led them through a columned hall that opened into a great domed room with a high ceiling. Torches flared on pillared walls, reflected by a pool of water that took up most of the floor.

The marmot bowed upon entering and bade them do the same. Rosamond resolutely refused, and Jennifer followed suit. He bared his teeth in deep displeasure.

"Pig!" Jennifer said aloud. "Brute! Rodent! Murderer!" It felt good to say it again.

He leapt at her, his teeth still bared.

"Down, cur!" said a voice behind them. It was the great El Ai, dressed in a pink silk morning gown and accompanied by a troop of guards. "Who mars these maids, mars my pleasure."

"They would not bow to the Lady Lyra," James replied.

The great El Ai waved off this complaint. "They will bow to me—that is enough."

Jennifer, meanwhile, now that they had stepped into the

high domed room, saw what James was talking about. This
was a temple, a sanctuary. The pool was filled with their lan-
guishing naiads, floating about like so many fallen aspen
leaves. Arranged on each long side of the pool were solemn
women in white robes.

"Ah," said El Ai, striding up to the edge of the water, "how
are my pretty priestesses?"

The white-robed women kept their eyes on a pedestal at
the far end. On it stood the beautiful woman of Jennifer's
dreams. She was crimson-gowned, red-lipped, with raven-dark
hair falling across her bare white shoulders. At her feet was a
raised altar, and lying upon it was the bloodied and barefoot
body of William. Jennifer saw all of this at once, and gasped.

El Ai instructed his guard to stay at the door, and following
James, he took both women by the arm and guided them
around the pool past the strangely immobile priestesses. As
they drew closer to Lady Lyra, Jennifer realized that the
woman was indeed a statue, just as Rosamond had
said—beautifully painted, arms and chin and eyes like life, but
only a statue nonetheless. The goddess within was after all the
goddess without, and merely made of stone at that. William,
though still, was quietly breathing, apparently whole and
undisturbed since she had seen him days ago in the hollow
cedar by the river. When she got quite close she saw, however,
that his heels had been hideously chewed.

The four of them stopped in front of the altar. El Ai
advanced himself a little and ostentatiously fell to his knees.
Jennifer saw that this crushed the curled toes of his satin slippers. She looked down at the top of his skull and marveled at
his utter baldness; his head reflected the light of the torches
that sputtered quietly on the walls. She thought to herself that
at this moment she should have been filled with fear of him,
or with pity for William, but no—she was thinking on crushed
slippers and bald crowns.

The great El Ai spread out his arms before the statue and made his petition:

> *"Thou, Nature, art my goddess; to thy law*
> *My services are bound. Accept the blood*
> *Of this thy sacrifice and hear the praise*
> *Of these from Otium we bring to thee."*

He arose then. Judging by what he had just said, Jennifer wondered if she and Rosamond would now be required to speak. And how could they, now that he had made it clear that William was to be murdered at last before their eyes? Instead of turning to them, however, El Ai walked to the lip of the pool and summoned the naiads.

"It is now your time," he said to them. "I trust that you are refreshed from your journey. Sing to us one of the songs of Amoenas. Do it for my sake, and for the sake of your supreme goddess, the Lady Lyra."

Reluctantly the naiads grouped themselves in the water, their sorrowful faces emerging as one. The dawn was breaking through windows in the entrance hall and lent a pallor to their cheeks. They would not face the great El Ai or the Lady Lyra, but resolutely turned their eyes to the north and west toward the distant land of the Three Queens. A wordless harmony sprang up among them, mournful in a minor key. Then words came, song came:

> *"By the waters of El Ai we sat down and wept*
> *When we remembered shining Amoenas.*
> *On the dry sands there we laid down our lyres,*
> *For there our captors required our praise.*
>
> *"How shall we sing the song of Love in a strange land?*
> *If we forget thee, Tower of Otium,*
> *Let our hands know pain and withering.*

> *Let our tongues cleave black to our mouths*
> *If we do not set Otium above highest joy.*
>
> *"Remember, O sisters, the men of El Ai,*
> *And how they swept upon us by night,*
> *Who sought in their souls to destroy the Tower,*
> *Who said in their hearts, 'Rase it, rase it!'*
>
> *"O daughter of the Beast, you devastator!*
> *Happy shall he be who requites you*
> *With that which you have done to us!*
> *Happy he who takes and dashes*
> *Your little one against the ax!"*

The song ceased with cruel abruptness, and the naiads melted back into the water. El Ai was rigid with rage, and even James had heard well enough to know the last blessing was meant for him.

"Little one indeed!" he snarled, puffing out the full bulk of his hoary chest. "The dawn has come and it is time."

From under the altar he pulled out a dagger with both paws. The hilt was long and the blade was longer. Solemnly he stood up and passed the knife to El Ai. The man stepped up to William's body on the altar, and the priestesses began to chant:

> *"I love El Ai, I love El Ai*
> *and honor and obey his goddess,*
> *The Lady Lyra, within us all."*

El Ai raised the dagger over William's chest. His hand quivered, perhaps from his rage at the song of the naiads, perhaps from some remaining drop of the bittersweet milk of human kindness. Jennifer wanted to scream, to charge, to throw herself biting and kicking at the shoulders of the big bald man, but she stood unable to do anything at all, no less fixed than the statue itself.

"Let it fall!" urged James. "Do it, sire, and in the heat! It is blood well spent."

But woe to him who severs the heart, thought Jennifer.

"My lord!" came a voice. There were rapid footsteps in the hallway.

El Ai turned in an irritated daze. The ranked guards at the door of the temple opened up and allowed a ragged messenger to step up to the brink of the bath.

"The watch reports an advance against us. Fires quenched, pools dried up, the walls of the city soon to be threatened."

"That shall never be," said El Ai. But he let the dagger drop to the floor as if it should, and looked about vacantly. "The prophesy is that El Ai shall never fall until the wood of the Dark Divide shall come against us. And how should it ever? The Dark Divide is a desert away. And trees do not walk. And should they decide to, I send my woodsmen to prevent them with the edge of the ax. Say again, messenger. Bring honest news, or by the Beast I will sheathe this dagger in your heart." He picked up the weapon and held it like an obscene gesture over the water.

"The watch does not lie, my lord. And I among them—from the top of the gate I have seen them coming massed against us, rooting and writhing as no men move, bringing with them the shade of death. They are oak trees, my lord. Live oaks from the Dark Divide."

The great El Ai grew suddenly pale. He turned toward the altar, then started toward the pool again. "Remain here with the captives, James. You, my guards, come with me. Raise your fellows. We shall see what tales these be. Even now our ax is laid to the root of the trees. Every one shall be cut down and cast in the fire. Oaks indeed! Tumbleweeds, and a drunken watch. Come, away. I shall be back."

He strode out of the temple then, and his guards with him.
Rosamond grasped Jennifer's hand, and they stood very still in
the menacing presence of the marmot. The sanctuary was
quiet except for the murmuring of the priestesses:

> "I love El Ai, I love El Ai
> And honor and obey his goddess,
> The Lady Lyra, within us all.

> "I love El Ai, I love El Ai
> And—"

"Oh, stuff it!" said a voice. "If I've heard that once, I've
heard it a thousand times here. You can't really love that
mountain of flesh, nor this place neither, by what I've seen of
it. Don't think for a minute you're convincing yourselves or me
or anyone else by heaping up these empty phrases. So be done
with it, and—Rosamond!"

It was Colin, of course, and Ronald by his side, standing
now in the entrance of the temple. They fairly flew past the
priestesses, who did in fact desist in their praises. Colin carried
a woodman's ax, and Ronald an ice ax that Jennifer thought
looked strangely familiar. The silver head of the ax burned
bright like the coal in her dream that Stella held in her outstretched hands.

Before Ronald and Colin could reach the altar, the marmot
sprang for Colin's throat. Colin dodged, and James plowed
snarling into the wall. Colin turned, ax ready, and the marmot
recoiled himself by a column. There Colin kept him at bay–the
marmot ready to spring again, and Colin ready to chop him out
of the air if he did.

Which left Ronald and the ice ax free and clear. He
approached the two women in slow amazement and did not
even say hello–which was typical of him, Jennifer thought. He
paused with them beside the altar, and then as if put in mind

of a promise, a vow made, he stepped around to the base of the statue and regarded it with a curious intensity, hefting the ice ax in his hands. The statue looked on as coldly as ever, the pale forehead, the hard green eye, the bitter lip possessing still an inert power.

"Lady Lira," Ronald said, "or Lady Lyra—whatever your name is—this time you're gone for good." He lifted the ax high and it trembled, just as the dagger had trembled over William's heart.

"Ronald," Jennifer softly implored, "let me." She had followed him around the altar. "It was me she ensnared. It was I who plucked the rose and the ax. I have the strength of a woman's hands. Let her suffer at mine, not yours."

Something in what Jennifer said awoke an echo in Ronald's mind. He lowered the ax and offered it with both hands to her, a sacred gift.

"Now," said Jennifer, "step back." She gazed at the statue sorrowfully and held the ice ax at her side. The painted eyes were proud and compelling. Even now they tried to enlist her loyalty. But Jennifer merely shook her head. Behind the glittering eyes she saw the vacant stare of the withered crone.

"Come out, sweet Lira," Jennifer called. "You may still come out from the belly of the Beast." She hardly knew what they were, these words she remembered from her dreams, but she knew they were the right ones to say. "Be no longer the goddess that you never were. Be no longer the goddess within, and know the mercy from without. Know that you are loved, and live."

As she uttered these words, Jennifer reached the head of the ax as high as she could till the sharpest point of the burning pick was just touching the lips of the statue. At first nothing happened. "Come out, sweet Lira," Jennifer pleaded. "Come out, sweet Lira, be married today."

With those words a tear formed in the hard green eye of

the statue and trickled down its painted cheek. Then one from the other eye. And another tear, and many more. The eyes blinked, warm and lovely.

"Come out, sweet Lira," Jennifer called. "It is required you do awake your faith."

The red lips opened against the ax, like the flowering of a cold budded rose. "Oh," they sighed. "I am a woman of unclean lips."

From next to the wall the marmot snarled, and Colin threatened him with his ax.

"By this ice ax," Jennifer said, "and by the Spirit of the One who made it, who planted the ash and buried the silver and shaped the hands by which it is made, those lips are cleansed."

"Oh," said the statue, "Oh," and shuddered, releasing itself from the bondage of stone. And then the statue truly and fully came alive, stepping off the pedestal and into the arms of Jennifer, flesh upon flesh, and they wept together. And Rosamond joined them, and they wept all three.

Ronald stood by awkwardly, and Colin glanced back as best he could to try to make out what was happening. But he didn't want the marmot to escape or to spring, either one. Finally Lira, still weeping and clinging close to Jennifer and Rosamond, made her way to Colin's side to address her marmot. Even off her pedestal she stood a full head higher than Colin.

"My marmot," she said simply. "James."

"What?"

"My poor corrupted marmot whom I have known from youth, when you faithfully joined me in the meadows, my constant companion in wickedness, even to my morning of death, I wake now to find you here, faithful still to my erring spirit. Be you faithful still, and join your mistress in life at last. Suffer this little one, this daughter of God, to touch your lips with the ax of my sister, even as she has touched mine. Let it be so, James. There is mercy at last, and you may share it."

The marmot snarled sullenly and grew very still. Jennifer slowly held out the ax, guiding the edge of the silver adze toward his curled lips. For a moment he sat quietly, as if to receive some transformation. But at the last instant, before the ice ax reached his lips, he sprang with a snarl at Jennifer. Before he got there Colin's ax sang through the light and sliced the marmot's head from its body in midair. Jennifer had hardly had a chance to recoil before the marmot lay bestrewn and beheaded at her feet. As they watched in silence, the blood ran over the floor before them and poured into the flashing pool.

"I'm sorry," said Colin, addressing himself to Lady Lira.

"It is as he has chosen," she replied. "And, I fear, as I have long ago chosen for him.

> *"Happy he who takes and dashes*
> *My little one against the ax!*

"The blessing is yours to keep, Colin. The mystery of wrath within grace. He kills only to make alive. We trust he shall. You have my love.

"And you, William," said Lady Lira, turning now to the body on the altar, "you too are now as I have wished, and how can I say I am sorry for it? Ah, do you smile? Do you smile at me in your wounded sleep? Look! Look there! It warms my new-thawed heart that you do so."

She bent over William's face and wept, drying it with her raven hair. The others gathered around the body and saw that William indeed wore a peaceful smile of gentle contentment.

When Lady Lira had finished weeping, she cradled William in both her arms and picked him up from off the altar. Then she turned and addressed the priestesses. "You who stand there night and day to say you honor and obey me, obey me now. Each of you reach into the pool and bear up a naiad in your arms and carry her after me out of this temple, even as I carry with me this worthy man."

The priestesses who had watched their goddess come to life without so much as batting an eye now suddenly bestirred themselves to lend their helping hands to the naiads. Soon each of them stood with a willowy water nymph in her arms, ready to follow at command.

"Which way?" said Lady Lira to Colin.

"Our horses are by the door in the wall just north of the western gate," Colin replied.

She nodded and led the way out of the temple and down the hall, striding smartly with William lying across her arms like a precious burden. Colin and Rosamond, Ronald and Jennifer followed them out, arms entwined, no less precious to each other, and behind them dozens of white-robed women, arms dripping with perhaps the sweetest burdens of all. They left in their wake a pedestal without a goddess, an altar without a sacrifice, the headless carcass of a hoary marmot, and a pool that flashed blood-red in the dying torches pale against the light of morning.

18

THEY FOUND THE STAIRWAY and courtyard deserted and passed through the gate of the palace into the streets of El Ai. Jennifer could hear shrieks of rage and hollow trampings far off, from the walls of the city and beyond, but El Ai itself was as sullen and quiet as it had been the evening before. The same dark people crouched in their doors beside their fires, turning their eyes on the strange troop of passersby as if a one-time goddess bearing a body, two young couples arm in arm, and a company of white-robed acolytes dripping with naiads were not at all a remarkable sight.

With Colin's guidance, Lady Lira led them to a door in the wall at the end of a dim and crooked alley. Men on the ramparts next to the western gate nearby were shouting and pointing, but not at the escaping party. Once through the door, on the cityside bank of the riverbed, Jennifer saw what excited the lookouts. Across the river, spread about the suburban plain, great live oaks were afoot in the land. They advanced improbably on their roots, crushing houses, sucking up pools, beating out fires with limbs the length of mountain crevasses. The inhabitants fled in terror before them, though one band led by the great El Ai was attacking the trees with spears and arrows that stuck in the trunks and dangled there, to little effect. One tree alone remained quietly rooted, shading a spot just over the river. Jennifer did not recall its being there the evening before. Hitched to its trunk were six saddled horses.

At a word from Colin, Lady Lira led them down the crumbling bank, across the sandy wash of the river, and back up to the tree and the horses. She laid her burden at its roots and put her face to the bark of the trunk, speaking low. Then she paused as if listening for the oak tree to speak in return. Satisfied, she turned and straightened, addressing herself to the priestesses who stood obediently behind them.

"Thus far, my daughters, you have served me with constant if misdirected love. I now release you from that service. Lay down your burdens next to mine at the foot of this great fatherly oak, and go your ways, never to praise Lady Lyra again except to remember the morning she was resurrected. If you wish to partake in her redemption, to devote yourself to the rushing water across the desert, I invite you now to share in our journey. This oak tree and his brothers will bear you, along with the naiads you have borne. If you cannot bring yourself to this journey, the way is clear to return to the city across the river and through the door. Only, the time is short, and once inside, I bid you stay away from the walls. The choice is yours; I no longer can make it for you."

The white-robed priestesses looked perplexed. All about the city walls the marauding oak trees tramped closer and closer, and streams of people were clogging the bridge and crowding into the western gate. All of a sudden, as if by a signal prearranged, the priestesses turned and fled as one, scrambling down the bank in a flurry and sprinting across the riverbed to the door in the wall, their white robes billowing out behind them. At first Jennifer thought they had all left. But when she looked at her companions again she saw that four of the priestesses—the youngest and strongest—remained among them.

"You have chosen well," Lady Lira said, and gave to each of them her hand. The four young women kneeled and touched their foreheads to the ground, but Lady Lira lifted them up. "You are not my priestesses; I am not your goddess. Together we are sisters in brokenness. We must learn to love each other well in the love of him in whom we live and have our being. More I will tell you. This much now."

Colin meanwhile had untied the horses. The army of oaks had completed their work of devastation outside the city and were now drawn up to left and to right on the bank of the river, encircling the walls as far as Jennifer could see. The gates were shut, the ramparts empty, the people all pent up inside. The rustling limbs of the long row of trees cast pleasant shade in the morning light that was already hot on the desert plain. Jennifer could half imagine a shallow river stealing beneath them, the calling of herons and croaking of frogs, and leisurely picnics enjoyed by the few who might belong to such a place.

As this prospect crossed her mind a strange thing began to happen. At first she heard just a quiet patter, like the falling of leaves, or dewdrip on a foggy morning. Then it increased to a gentle rain, trickling down from twigs and branches as off the edges of great umbrellas. What began as a drizzle progressed to a torrent. Not only the crowns but also the roots of hundreds of trees began to gush great streams of water, sucked out of the many harbored pools and now disgorged in a thousand cascades down the bone-dry bank of the river and into the long-neglected channel. The water merely collected at first, or sank in the soil, but soon a river began to rise, spreading silty and deep from bank to bank, and moving in a mighty current between the city and the desert.

Jennifer squeezed Ronald's arm. She whispered to him,

> "Dark brown is the river,
>   Golden is the sand.
> It flows along forever,
>   With trees on either hand."

"On one hand, anyway," Ronald said.

Jennifer smiled. The Amoenas had trees on both hands, but it was green. She wondered when life would ever imitate poetry with complete precision.

At last the trees had given all the water they had. The river was filled to the very brim, and the sandstone bridge that linked the desert to the gate began to melt away in the current, falling apart in chunks and shards until nothing at all was left of it. Jennifer was overjoyed to see it go. Now they could depart in peace, untroubled by fear of pursuit.

But the oaks had one more task to complete before they left. Suddenly the tree they were under gave itself voice and shouted, "Now!" It clashed its limbs together like drums, like the mighty clapping of giant hands. The other trees took up the shout all up and down the desert river, beating their long stout limbs together in thunderous arboreal applause. "Now! Now!" Jennifer covered her ears in the din, and her insides shook, and the ground trembled. And all at once the tall deserted walls of the city tumbled outward and buried themselves in the depths of the river. The splash that went up over the desert soaked Jennifer and Ronald and all, and the trees stood clapping and glistening wet, shouting for joy.

The devastation was complete. The houses and fires and pools were gone, and now the wall, leaving only a sandstone palace square in the midst of terrible squalor. Crowded in amongst the hovels were the outlying desert dwellers, looking rather ill at ease among the darker citizens. Jennifer wondered if those who said they loved El Ai and those who hated it in their hearts would now come to some agreement about the place as a *place*, a watered nook beneath desert hills, a quiet land of little rain that might yet blossom as the modest rose it was meant to be. For Jennifer, it could never afford the pleasure of Otium, but she realized it was no wasteland either.

Even as she caught sight of the great El Ai and his band of guards, staring blankly back at them from what used to be the western gate, she wished him well, hoping he would learn to dwell contentedly in the land in which he found himself. She could hardly help feeling pity for him. He looked dazed and foolish—and frightened too when he saw Lady Lira standing among them. The erstwhile goddess held up her hand to wish him peace, but instead of responding he turned with his men and fled towards his palace, trampling and shoving his masses to get there.

"I hope we see no more of *him*," said Jennifer to Ronald. "You have no idea how disgusting he was to Rosamond—to me even."

Ronald only smiled shyly and brushed some oak leaves from her hair.

Lady Lira stooped and lifted William in her arms again. Colin mounted one horse, Ronald another, and Rosamond and Jennifer climbed up behind them. This conveniently left a horse apiece for the white-robed women, who were looking askance at the trees around them as possible modes of transport. When the horses and people had moved aside, the fatherly dryad let down his limbs and caught up the naiads into his crown, nestling them with the mistletoe. Then they all set off at an easy pace, Lady Lira and William in the lead.

The sun was high, but Jennifer felt the welcome shade of the oak tree marching along behind them, and then the shade of many oaks, the delicious cool of a movable forest traveling with them across the desert. Birds called and swooped in the branches, and the naiads sang a song of blessing:

> "We lift our eyes to the Dark Divide:
> Return is sweet to the place of help.
> Swift are the roots of them that bear us
> To green bright waters."

Though Jennifer had hardly slept, the shade of the oaks and the song of the naiads so soothed her soul that the journey that day across the desert filled her with a strange and pleasing exhilaration. Ronald, she thought, must have been no less exhausted, but as she held him tight in the saddle she had no sense that he was tired. They exchanged many words in the long day's ride, but none unkind.

When evening came they caught sight of a campfire in a barren place at the very foot of the Dark Divide. "I have an idea whose that is," Colin said. As they approached, they saw four figures run from the fire and dive under a nearby wagon. "Woodcutters," Ronald told Jennifer. "We borrowed their horses. Perhaps now we can borrow something to eat. This music has done very little to fill my stomach."

They stopped their horses next to the fire. Lady Lira lay William down, and the forest of oaks dispersed themselves to their time-honored places and took root. The fatherly oak remained near the fire, though far enough from it to keep the naiads from discomfort. Over the flames hung an iron kettle on a makeshift tripod. Ronald and Jennifer dismounted and tested the broth. "Delicious," they murmured. "Almost as good as Chambers'."

Colin, meanwhile, marched to the wagon with ax in hand and flushed the woodcutters into the open. "We thank you for your horses," he said, "and crave the use of them one day longer. In the meantime, we ask part of your supper, and blankets for the night." He held the ax in a menacing fashion as he spoke, so that the woodcutters, shivering with fear in the firelight, had very little choice in the matter.

"You speak much too haughtily, Colin." It was Lady Lira, who had come up beside him. At sight of her the woodcutters fell to the ground in absolute terror, pointing to their necks as if asking Colin to dispatch them then and there with his ax.

"They are from El Ai," Colin explained. "They came to destroy the grove of my father. I owe no more courtesy than I give." He sounded resentful, but also embarrassed.

"They are from El Ai," Lady Lira repeated. "And no less are you, O son of the south, your mother a priestess refugee from the very temple in which these women thought to serve me day and night. Methinks these men would make fit consorts for my women. As those may learn to worship aright, these may learn to care for what they cut before. Forgive them, Colin. They served El Ai with blind hearts and knew not what they did. Mercy triumphs over judgment. If for me, how much more for the least of these."

The four men slowly lifted their heads, and Colin slowly lowered his ax. The former priestesses quietly gathered on either side of Lady Lira, and one by one and pair by pair she raised the woodsmen from the ground and put their hands in the hands of the women. It was done in a moment of holy silence. Jennifer thought she had never seen such a good and pleasant unity.

Those newly joined came back to the fire, and blankets were spread, and stew was served, and tales were told, and songs were sung, and the women danced. Along about midnight one of the woodcutters told a joke about their grandfather (for as it turned out, they were four young brothers). Colin asked the name again and said it sounded somewhat familiar, and when Colin told them his mother's name the four woodcutters leapt as one, saying that this was their long-lost aunt, sister to their departed father, who had often told them she had been killed by the spirits of evil trees in the wild. The upshot was that the brothers and Colin embraced each other and wept on each other's necks as cousins.

This surprising reunion was still in progress when one live limb of the fatherly oak took Colin aside. Colin seemed to confer with the knots of the trunk, and returned to the fire with a serious look. "My friends and cousins," he called to them.

Their laughter died.

"My father tells me he feels in his roots the fast approach

of many horses. The great El Ai has found a way across his river and is come in wrath to reclaim his captives. We must on tonight, over the Dark Divide in the stars, and make our stand at Otium. Our friends the oaks must keep their roots—we cannot ask them to do again what they can perform but once in a century. Only, my father shall accompany us to carry the naiads and guard the rear of our company. Rest is sweet, but the valley of the Amoenas is sweeter." As he finished his urging he poured a bucket of water on the fire, and it hissed and steamed in the light of the moon.

Jennifer was dreadfully vexed at the prospect of another night ride. She had been dreamily leaning her head on Ronald's shoulder, nearly ready to stretch out on the ground and sleep. But she got to her feet like everyone else, and helped find the horses tethered out in the wild oats, and got up behind Ronald on the chestnut mare they had ridden that day across the desert. Colin and Rosamond mounted too, and the four new couples had a horse to each. Lady Lira regathered William in her arms, and the oak tree took up the sleeping naiads. The strength of the oak tree Jennifer could understand, but the stamina of Lady Lira all that day and now tonight was beyond her.

Then they were off, swift and silent, climbing through the dark tangle of manzanita up the reaches of the divide. In an hour they came to a rocky knoll from which they could look out over the desert. Colin saw a flash and churn approaching their camp, a column of horses, and pointed it out to all the rest. Jennifer breathed quiet thanks they were not on that

darkling plain
Swept with confused alarms of struggle and flight.

It was bad enough being just one hour ahead in the hills.

Lady Lira led them on with tireless strides, easily keeping

ahead of the horses which panted and sweated beneath double burdens. Cottonwoods gleamed in quiet ravines, and higher up, moon-pale aspen quivered in the deep night breeze. The way became rocky, and pines appeared, and sometimes giant sugar cones came whooshing down around their ears like stones from space. When they got to the tarn at the top of the ridge, a faint rim of dawn shone over the desert. The horses were staggering with fatigue, and the couples dismounted to drink and rest. The oak tree stood incongruously on the very pass, his twisted arms magnificently spread against the folds and dikes of shattered rock. Colin went to speak with him and reported back that his father complained of the thin air.

"But it's down from here," he reassured everyone, "and we've got to be farther ahead of them now than we were before." He no sooner spoke than they heard the sound of clattering stones from just over the pass behind them. Colin shot back up to the oak and uttered a groan.

The others did not even ask. They leapt to the backs of their tired horses and plunged down the hill, Lady Lira in the lead and Colin and Rosamond riding last by the lumbering oak. The moonlight was barely sufficient to show them the way through rocky defiles, and once they gained the hemlock forest it was dark indeed beneath the trees. Had the trail not been soft and wide, they would surely have ridden themselves to disaster. Lady Lira called a warning for every switchback, and they wheeled each one at improbable speeds. Jennifer gripped with her tired knees as best she could, but at every turn she felt herself nearly flung headlong into outer shapes of trunks and darkness.

Down, down, down they swirled, weaving back and forth through the forest till first light reached this side of the mountain, and ferns and lichen began to show themselves in a blur. At last they reached the rim of the gorge, and Lady Lira came to a halt. "We can't stop!" said Colin, galloping up. And then they all saw why she had.

The sun was on the point of rising just over the head of the canyon, there at the brink of the great falls. In its gathering light they could see across to the small split summit of the Tower of Otium, hovering in empty air above the center of the gorge. And standing on the downriver half of the summit, looking intently across the chasm into the eyes of Lady Lira, was the lone robed figure of Garth himself, no less statuesque than she had been on her pedestal in the desert temple. He held William's ice ax in his hand, lifting it high in solemn greeting. Jennifer could not make out his face from this distance, but she studied the profile of Lady Lira's and thought she saw there mingled parts of shame and longing. What Lady Lira might have said or wanted to say, Jennifer was ever afterwards curious to know. As it was, Lady Lira merely stood in her long red gown, soiled with travel, holding out William in her arms as if to offer restitution. Then Garth nodded, and Lady Lira nodded back, as if they had reached some final agreement or exchanged a mutual permission. The first rays of light broke over the canyon and caught the head of the upraised ax in a flash of fire that soon enveloped Garth's face and beard.

"Now!" he shouted. His voice rang and echoed across the gorge, even as they began to hear the pounding of horses above and behind them. With both his hands and all his might Garth pulled the ax back over his shoulder and brought it arcing over his head in a smashing blow to the pedestal of the second summit. A few small rocks split off and clattered away to the canyon depths. But Jennifer sensed that something greater than this had happened. Far away, from the head of the river, there came a sound as if the earth itself had groaned. A muffled surge, a sinking, a roar—and the ledge beneath them trembled slightly.

"It is the dolorous stroke," Lady Lira turned and told them, "and we must go."

A yell went up from the mountain above them, and they saw El Ai in the morning light, cutting straight downhill across the switchbacks with dozens of horsemen on either side. They did not wait for him to arrive. Lady Lira plunged into the alder ravine, and the horses after, the oak tree crashing behind them as best he could. "I am sorry, my cousins, you must pardon me," he kept saying to the alder thickets. "I must crush your trunks for a greater cause. Let us pass, and cross yourselves against the hooves of those who follow."

Jennifer felt branches swat her right and left as their horse careened the quick-turning trail. It was rather like falling down a spiral staircase and being beaten with whips and cords the entire way. But she did not mind—she was mostly afraid of falling off, which seemed somehow more terrifying in the light than it had in the darkness.

As they descended, the sunrise moved with them down the ravine, as if they were bringing the dawn to the floor of the canyon. They could hear the curses of El Ai behind them, he and his horsemen hacking and slashing with swords and axes through the alder. The horse that Jennifer and Ronald were riding was starting to limp, as if it had lamed itself with exertion. They urged it on, but soon found themselves next to the dryad behind the others, and hearing more and more clearly the imprecations that El Ai poured out upon Lady Lira and the Lava Beast and the Spirit of Otium—as if he had no steady view as to what he swore by or swore against.

At last the trail began to level in cedar trees beside the brook, and the oak tree was saying, "Pardon me, my brothers, a thousand pardons," as he snapped off the cedar limbs in his way. Ronald and Jennifer emerged from the grove on the brink of the river and saw the others already crossing the thin stone bridge. Their limping horse took one look at the narrow span and put each hoof to a full lame halt. "Move it!" cried Ronald. "We're almost there!" But the horse stayed put. They could hear El Ai come galloping up and slash at the oak tree right behind them. "Please!" said Jennifer, wondering what one said to a horse in a time like this. (*Giddyup* sounded too prosaic.) She made as to threaten with her ax. But the horse wouldn't move.

Ronald leapt to the ground and pulled Jennifer with him. They ran at full speed onto the bridge and sprinted as hard as they possibly could to the other side. Lady Lira was there to greet them. She had laid William down on the bank, and told them to follow the others to the cottage.

"You're staying?" said Ronald. "Shouldn't we all?"

"You must go with the others," Lady Lira commanded. "It is expedient that one should be sacrificed for many. This is my time."

Jennifer looked at William on the ground. Lady Lira said to her, "He too is in my charge. You must go, and go quickly."

She no sooner had spoken than El Ai and his band of horsemen came swarming around the oak to the bridge. They had mauled the trunk and hacked away some smaller limbs, and the wail of naiads rent the air. Lady Lira advanced to meet them, resolute, entirely alone. Ronald and Jennifer turned and fled.

Soon they reached the others at the cottage, high above the narrow bridge. Their boat had been placed there, right on the doorstep beside the spring, and gathered around it were squirrels and raccoons and weasels and deer—even a mother bear and her cubs—as if all of them had come to flee El Ai as well. As curious as this assembly was, Ronald and Jennifer did not think to ask about it. They stood solemnly next to Colin and Rosamond, side by side with a pair of deer–antlered buck and glossy doe–and looked back at the bridge below them. It was still in shade, though the sun now shone on the cottage and the entire tower.

What Jennifer saw was Lady Lira standing face to face with the great El Ai, who had dismounted at the center of the bridge. They couldn't have been six feet apart. Lady Lira, tall and severe, was saying something with great firmness. She had no weapon, but El Ai was threatening her with a long cruel knife. From a distance it looked like the one he had wielded next to the altar. Half his men were lined up behind him; the other half were still tormenting the oak on shore. Jennifer realized it had been their horse that had kept the tree from gaining the bridge. The thought make her stomach weak.

Colin was stamping and tearing at his hair. "Why did I let her persuade me up here? Of all the shame—for a son to stand by and to watch his father dishonored like this. O woe, woe, woe and shame upon my head!"

He wrenched himself free from Rosamond's arms and ran partway down the path—and stopped. The sun had reached the crown of the oak, and the guard was bent on toppling the whole tree into the river. On the bridge, El Ai had edged closer to Lady Lira, probing the narrowing space between them with his knife. But Colin was no longer looking at the pair on the bridge or at his father. He was looking upstream, as the rest of them at the cottage were too.

From behind the nearest bend in the canyon they heard a roar like nothing their ears had heard before. Thunder could only dimly suggest it. The roar filled the canyon from wall to wall, onrushing, growing louder and louder like the deep increase of a kettledrum. Ronald gripped Jennifer's arm and shouted one long word in her ear: "*Jokulhlaup.*" He was the only one that knew.

And then it was upon them—a wall of water and ice and stones and snags some thirty feet high, bearing down on the Tower of Otium like the alpine tidal wave it was. Colin just had time to sprint back to the cottage before it broke on the thin stone bridge in the first rays of the risen sun. The great El Ai was still flourishing his dagger, and Lady Lira standing fearlessly over him, and then they were gone, obliterated by the shock and thunder of the surge. The water smashed to the very doorstep where Jennifer and the others stood, and then rolled by in a giant flood, rich with earth and jagged icebergs, clashing rocks and whole red cedars torn by their roots. One old giant, curiously hollow and blackened at the base, came abruptly to rest in the deluged meadow before the cottage. Jennifer brushed its mangled side, its shattered limbs, and heard the dryad of her dream: *The river gives its life for me, and I shall give my life for the river. Gladly I shall lay it down.*

Where the bridge had been there was nothing to see. El Ai and his horses and men were crushed and drowned and washed away. But the oak tree, the naiads, Lady Lira, and the body of William were no less buried and gone. A strange calm came upon all God's creatures in front of the cottage as the noise of the *jokulhlaup* pounded away from them down the canyon. They stood looking out over muddy waters, the floor of the gorge made formless and void. Colin was weeping. Jennifer clung to the neck of the doe and to Ronald's side, and found that her cheeks were streaming with tears.

19

FOR THE REST of that day they rather gloomily set about fixing up the cottage. The four woodcutters were fortunately just as good at joining together tables and beds as they were at chopping trees apart. The women helped Rosamond put her kitchen to rights again, and by evening the cottage was much as it was before El Ai and his mounted guard had brought it to ruin.

Jennifer had half expected Garth to come and lend some cheer to the strain of their survivorship. But all day long they saw neither ax nor beard of him. Even Rosamond, thinking on her hopes of a wedding, was put out that Garth did not show himself. "After all," she said, "he got up, he can get down." So while she and Colin readied some supper, Ronald and Jennifer stepped outside to look about the tower and the island.

The renewed order within the cottage was foiled by the chaos without. The waters had receded, and the terraces that led down through the shadows were choked with boulders and debris. Torn trees and snags jutted this way and that out of layers of mud like leaning corpses. The thin stone bridge to the south was gone, and in the water below them a giant logjam butted up against the head of the island. As far upstream as they could see, the verdant shores of the pleasant Amoenas had been massacred as if by winter avalanche.

"What a mess," breathed Ronald. "What a sorry mess." He thought to himself that the canyon might as well be dammed and inundated, if only to cover the wounds from sight.

"But look here," said Jennifer, "this *is* curious." She pointed to the washed-up cedar beside them, prostrate for its giant length, its roots appealing in withered agony to the sky. The bubbling spring flowed sweet and clear from the doorstep into the hollow of the tree, and growing from the bark were tiny seedlings, green and tender against the firescarred frame of millennia. The log was nurse to resurrections of its glory, giving itself in death to life. There was promise here, no less than in Noah's rainbow, and Jennifer felt strangely heartened by what she saw.

They took the familiar path round the tower, or what they could see of it through the debris, and found that the bridge to the north had held. Given its mass, Ronald was not at all surprised. As they stood regarding it, however, they were startled to see in the westering rays of the autumn sun the bald dome of a white-bearded man who was striding toward them across the arch. He was robed and fat, and when he climbed to meet them they both said, "Chambers!"

"Yes," he said. "The very same—unchanged, untransmutable in identity, and unimpeachable in name. One week older and a daylong worn in the soles of my boots. By the Beast, what a weary distance!" He sat on a stone and mopped his ample brow with a handkerchief.

"Came to check on the boat, of course—on little Amoenas—and on you all while I was at it. Saw the morning fracas in the pond and couldn't be sure there'd be anything left but food for salmon and slivers to sell for indulgences to credulous maids at midnight dances in the meadows."

"Your boat's up at the cottage, Sir Chambers. High and dry," Ronald said.

"You'll find supper there too," said Jennifer.

"Pleased to hear it, very pleased." He nodded to each of them. "I think I'll just proceed that way, if you'll excuse me. Journey's end is a good place to start, if that's where you're headed." He got up to go and added by way of afterthought, "You wouldn't have happened to see anything of Lady Demaris now, would you have?"

Jennifer shook her head. "Not for days. She seemed in a hurry. A very busy person, I think."

Chambers nodded. "That she is, yes indeed. An undeniably busy woman." He clucked his tongue and strode away to his boat and his supper without so much as saying good-bye—not that he'd really said hello.

Ronald and Jennifer smiled at each other, then joined hands and made their way down the trail to the cove. They noticed at once that the sandy beach, unlike the rest of the island, was as clean as ever. "Curiouser and curiouser," Jennifer said. Then it was Ronald's turn to point. The alder trees by the shore were gone, and in their place was a large live oak, not native to this northern place but flourishing here at the placid waterside nevertheless. The forest downcanyon was mowed with precision to an equal height on either side of the riverbank. But here was the oak, strangely misplaced and undeniably alive.

"Do you think . . . ?" said Jennifer, dropping his hand. Its spread of branches, long and thick, looked rather familiar. She approached and saw that every limb was scarred but intact. "It is!" she cried, and touched its bark in renewal of friendship, tracing her fingers all the way around the bole. And then she gasped.

Behind the oak, under lasting arms, lay the peaceful shape of a man on his back. "William," she whispered. He was resting there in the dying day as if not yet awakened from an overlong nap. They knelt beside him and felt his measured breath on their cheeks. His face was flush with newness of health, his clothes dry, his heels intact. The bandage was gone from around his temples, and no wound showed. "Touch his side," Jennifer whispered. Ronald gingerly undid the parka and felt the flesh. It was sweet and whole. He held his hand on the place and marveled.

The sun mellowed and ripened in lowland ridges of Douglas fir. The cove was alight, and out of the water sped quicksilver sounds of many voices. "The naiads!" said Jennifer. Their lovely faces encircled the sandbar that separated the cove from the river, and they filled the sky again and again with a shout of gladness:

> "We will sing unto the Lord,
>   for he has triumphed gloriously;
> The horse and rider thrown into the sea!"

The noise echoed off the tower and across the canyon like the aftershock of the flood itself, and Jennifer felt exultation in sound and sense of word upon word. She and Ronald remained on their knees beside the gloriously breathing body, and knew what they were thankful for.

When the last notes faded, and the naiads disappeared with the dusk, they both became aware at once that Garth was standing solemnly over them, ax in hand. "Welcome, children, and take heart," he said. There was an ancient weariness in his voice. "Let us bear the body back to the cottage. Tomorrow the wedding, and then a journey yet to go. You must row your friend down the rest of the stream to the Western Sea, and then your task shall be complete."

To Jennifer he looked sad as he spoke. It occurred to her that not everyone had been saved in the flood. She thought of the one on whom he might think, and felt his sorrow. As for Ronald, he was simply curious how Garth had contrived both to climb and descend the smooth face of the rock, and how the blow of a single ax might communicate its local power to the heft and thrust of a distant glacier. But he didn't ask.

The wedding took place at noon the next day on the sand of the cove, under the crown of the great live oak. Colin and

Rosamond stood in the shade in their best white clothes, with Ronald and Jennifer flanking them in knickers and smock. The four other couples had asked that morning if they might be married as well, but Garth had told them that Lady Lira had already joined them in word and deed when she had paired them hand in hand. ("They won't last long *here*," Colin whispered behind them. "The sort from El Ai—they can't stand the rain." To which Rosamond told him to be quiet and to try to show more courtesy on his wedding day.) Ronald and Jennifer, after much conferring on their part, had asked Garth the same hopeful question. Or rather, Ronald had asked in half-articulate syllables while Jennifer stood blushing by. But Garth had told them their mother and father must come to give witness and consent, and bade them wait. And so they did.

Garth conducted the ceremony with weighty words he read from a parchment, exhorting the newmade husband and wife to love and obedience, submission and authority. Jennifer watched to see which words were directed to which particular spouses, but it was never clear to whom exactly Garth was speaking at any one moment, and so she supposed that she and Ronald, like all those before them, would have to sort this out themselves. Chambers stood beaming among the four couples from El Ai, his cheer a counter to Garth's grave countenance. Behind him the boat lay victualed and waiting, with newcut oars that the woodsmen had fashioned from the cedar log in front of the cottage. And next to the boat lay William on the sand, booted and ready, as amenable as he had been at any moment of the last many days.

Garth pronounced a stolid amen, the oak tree clapped its limbs in joy, and Colin and Rosamond sweetly embraced in a shower of leaves. The new-married pair then said their farewells to Ronald and to Jennifer. The two women clasped and cried; the men shook hands and then thought better of it and hugged. Then the woodsmen and priestesses led Colin and

Rosamond back up the path to the other side of the Tower of Otium, there to hymn the blessing of the epithalamion at the threshold of the bridal cottage. As the procession climbed from the cove, the naiads re-emerged and sang, haunting the air yet one more time with the pure calm music of their voices:

> "This grassy terrace under the stone
> Is all we need, given our feet and October sun.
> The trail leads upward into the snowbreeze,
> Winter kiss in the green-pooled canyons."

A cool fall wind swept down the gorge as if in answer to invocation. The column of couples rounded the tower out of sight, and the sweet song faded and ceased.

Sooner than they thought possible, Ronald and Jennifer stood with Garth and Chambers beside them, ready to place the sleeping William back in the boat. It was as if they had never left the crystal chamber deep in the ice of the Mirror Glacier. The river glided pleasantly away from the cove, calling them of its own sweet will to renew the journey to the sea.

Patiently, Garth raised his arms and pronounced once more a benediction:

> "The tongues of sand and tide go with thee,
> The arms of the floating maiden support thee,
> The song of the ouzel lead thee aright,
> And may—"

Just here he was cut off by the very song of the ouzel he had named. It came winging upriver, out of the forested valleys below, calling *bzeet! bzeet!* as it skimmed the water. Then it landed on the prow of the boat and made its customary bows. Ronald looked at Jennifer. She wanted to smile, but Garth looked too solemn.

"And may thy voice find praise with these."

Garth took both axes out of the boat—the long one that
was William's, the short one that was Stella's once—and
turned to plunge them into the water. Jennifer supposed he
was about to change them to oars again, even though new
ones had been provided. But before the axes touched the river
he stopped and straightened in surprise. Garth looked downstream. The others looked with him.

"Well, I'll be blessed," said Chambers quietly.

Coming toward them, against the breeze and against the
current, was the silhouette of a small wooden barge. Small it
was, but large enough for three tall figures, crowned and
veiled, to stand side by side in the flat-squared prow. They
were female and feminine, greenclad in loose long gowns that
trailed in the breeze as the barge came on at the slow speed
of mystery. Ronald and Jennifer held each other's hands
tightly. Each of them sensed that something greater than the
waterfall was here. Nothing would become their journey
down the gorge so much as this the leaving of it. Chambers
mumbled beatifically. Garth just stared, his beard working in
consternation.

The barge came skimming over the shallows at the foot of
the cove, there where the naiads had sung by the sandbar, then
crossed the calm and nudged the beach beside the oak. The
three gowned women held absolute silence. Beneath crowns
and veils their hair was all that told them apart—golden,
auburn, raven black. The first stepped softly to the sand and
took the shorter ice ax from Garth. She lifted her veil and
Jennifer knew her for the merciful woman in the waterfall and
in her dream—Stella of the alpine stars, utterly lovely and
severe. The woman turned to Ronald and to Jennifer and
pierced them through with a gaze that was so achingly good
they could not bear it—but they wanted nothing more in the

world than to be able to bear it longer. She thrust the shaft of
the ax in the sand and left it upright just beneath their two
joined hands. Then she spoke:

> *"Nurture what is taken, restore what is thine.*
> *Friendship of opposition is ended;*
> *Contraries yield.*
> *You came in trouble, depart in peace."*

With measured step the second woman came ashore and
took the longer ax from Garth. She stooped beside William and
lifted her veil, and Jennifer saw it was Lady Demaris, lovely as
well, but suffused with kindness, a face of mercy less austere.
With the head of the ax she very gently touched his lips, then
laid it crosswise on his chest. And she too spoke:

> *"When you wake*
> *You shall know that stars fade,*
> *That night does not last,*
> *That the sorrows of planets*
> *Are the joys of morning,*
> *That birds repair and blossoms*
> *Kindle after darkness:*
> *Nature's first lesson,*
> *First hint, of grace."*

Lady Demaris kissed his forehead and called him by name.
"William, you have slept to know we accomplish more in our
mortal wounding than in our heroic designs. Yours has been
the better fortitude. Wake at last from things dying to things
newborn."

As she rose from beside him, a smile broke upon William's
lips. He stirred faintly, his eyes still closed.

"My sisters," said Garth, his voice quavering, "you have

spared us much trouble. Let us help you place the body on board so that you may bear him to final healing."

He stooped to lift William in his arms, but the two women checked him. Instead of reaching down to William they ranged themselves on each side of Garth and gently took him by the elbows. Softly and firmly they guided him up onto the barge and presented him there to the third woman, the tallest and strongest. He gazed at the figure solemnly, and then Stella and Lady Demaris removed the veil of Lady Lira, whose face was so contrite with tears that none ashore could keep from shedding more besides. She fell to her knees and clasped his thighs in supplication, but Garth reached down and slowly raised her to full height. His shoulders shook as Jennifer watched him from behind. "No cause," she heard him murmur aloud. "No cause."

When he turned to look back, the barge had already left the shore.

Chambers held up a hand of parting. "Good-bye," said Chambers brokenly. "Good-bye, my brother."

The barge crossed the cove to the bar, and Garth called back, "Let there be no sadness of farewell."

And then they receded down the current, the bearded old man, happy at last, and the three crowned sisters, queens indeed. Jennifer thought of the Fates in Ovid, three and terrible. But no, she decided—these were three as the gentle Graces, the minglers of beauty and forgiveness. And thus they remained, green-eyed and haunting, in Jennifer's mind to the end of her days.

Chambers' mind was apparently stayed on a single sister in particular. "One fine woman," he muttered distractedly. The barge was nearly out of sight. "Be a lucky man—" He cut himself off as if seized by a plan. While Ronald and Jennifer stood inert, he grabbed the two fresh cedar oars, tossed them in the boat, and shoved off into the cove.

"And where are *you* going?" called Ronald after him.

While the ouzel nodded from its perch on the bow, Chambers fitted the oars to the locks and sputtered the blades across the water in a frenzy of spectacular rowing. He reached the current just as the barge swept round a bend far down the river.

"*Festina lente!*" Chambers called back. "Hasten slowly, until you're late. And now I am. What I never was, that is." He threw up his oars in exasperation. "Chambers is willing. Who needs a pond when there is the sea?"

Ronald and Jennifer watched him diminish on the quickening current until the bend. And he was gone.

20

JENNIFER AND RONALD were left on the beach hand in hand. All was silent, and they watched the river. They lingered in the breath of parting, alone again and a part of all that they had met, and reassured by holy palm on holy palm in the touch of their flesh.

"I say!" said Jennifer suddenly. She felt the crowding of soft petals against their fingers.

Both of them looked and caught their breath. Planted anew and afresh between them, Stella's ax had bloomed again. A deep red rose had grown out of the burnished head and quietly enveloped their grasp.

It really is over then, Jennifer thought. *The healing is done.* They knelt to smell the reborn rose, to drink its scent, and Jennifer felt satisfied to leave it bending where it was.

"Hey!" called an anxious voice from behind them. "A little slack on this schrund here! Enough to get down this sunken bridge, if you think it will hold."

They turned to see William sitting up and holding his ice ax out before him as if to arrest an imminent fall. His eyes were open and peered without focus across the river.

"Slack! I said slack! What are you—" He gave a short cry and hurled himself chest first on the sand, digging in with ax and toes to make himself immovable.

"William," said Ronald. He leaned over and placed his

187

hands on the knuckles clenched along the ax. "I've got you. You can come out now."

William looked up and seemed to see him. Ronald slowly released his hold, and William his. He brushed his fingers across the sand and looked at the oak, the tower, the river.

"I have had a dream," he said to Ronald. "I have had a most rare vision."

"And so you have," Jennifer suggested, wanting to be noticed as well.

"Yet I am doubtful where I have been, and ignorant what place this is." He carefully stood and looked about at the walls of the gorge, appealing to them in familiar wonder.

Jennifer stepped closer to William to make herself known, but before she could utter a word of greeting she heard a voice more constant and normal to her ears than any save one in the quiet of the grave.

"Jennifer!" it called from a distance. "How's my girl? Looking splendid, both of you, really—and, William, what a pleasant and timely surprise."

They found themselves staring at the irrepressible Dr. Howe, who was striding across the sand of the cove as if coming to greet a host of visitors at his door.

"Dad!" she said uncertainly, meeting him with a modest hug. "How did—"

"A long day's push, I can certainly assure you. Down to Gwen's cabin and across the base of Center and South to that goatwalk on the face of these cliffs. I can almost see why Escee preferred to fly. But poor Escee—a dreadful occurrence just yesterday morning. Inspecting the snout of the eastern lobe by helicopter at the very moment the glacier gave way—he must have just touched down by the stream gauge. Not that he didn't have the facts from me, and a proper warning. But a terrible thing—loss of human life and all that. And he such a good sponsor—a real believer in the scientific enterprise." At this he blinked his bushy brows, truly touched by this saddest face of the tragedy.

"But the work must go on. Just as he'd have it. Nothing to do but hasten down here to inspect the damsite. And—oh, yes—at Gwen's this morning—she'd told me last week you'd all dropped down to her cabin for a visit. And she'd radioed later that one of you, at least, was ill, and we were so busy that all I could do was send our regrets. But this morning, when she said I'd find you here, I saw your instincts, stealing a march on the proper study of our cataclysmic aftermath. And what better place? The dam, of course, is out of the question, but think of the station for research we could put here. That high broad bench on the other side of this granidiorite monolith is the perfect site for a Quonset hut.

"Ronald," he continued, putting a fatherly arm on his shoulders, "you don't know what a delight it was to see a glacier *really* move. Nothing like a *jokulhlaup* to demonstrate my little notion of entropy in glacial systems, the self-destruction of regulated bodies of ice in the long term. So difficult to observe in a lifetime, but here we've seen it!—the resignation of a glacial regime to the ultimate laws of thermodynamics. We've got a whole autumn ahead of us here—the data can't wait until next summer."

"Here?" said Ronald.

"For science," said Dr. Howe. "As your advisor, let me suggest that for this semester you quit your books. Throw classes to the winds. Let the gorge be your school, and nature your teacher." He winked and nodded suggestively.

Ronald looked at Jennifer, and she slyly shrugged. "Dr. Howe," he said, "I like this place, and—"

"Splendid, my boy. Absolutely splendid. And William—dear me, how one forgets. When I dropped by your cabin just this morning I found your lovely wife in possession of a suckling babe. Her water broke yesterday just at dawn. Somewhat premature, she said, but delivered with the help of three charming women whose names I have unhappily forgotten. And completely in health, nothing whatever to worry about. I offer you my congratulations."

With that he shook the father's hand with all due heartiness. But he might as well have been operating a pump handle for all the response he got from William, who stared past him to greater heights of incomprehension.

"Well, what is it? A boy or a girl?" Jennifer demanded.

"Bless me," said Professor Howe, scratching his head. "She told me, I'm sure, but as it is I don't remember. So much going on. This unfortunate business of Escee, and the *jokulhlaup*, of course—a whole new field of research. We'll have to close up the high camp soon—or winterize it—construct a cabin above the lake perhaps. Leave a crew there to keep an eye on our galloping glacier and move our base to this lovely island—enough to do here to make use of our every minute."

". . . and willingly could waste my time in it," Ronald added, firmly grasping Jennifer's hand. They stood in front of the ax and the rose so that Dr. Howe could not possibly see it.

"Eh? What's that?" the professor said. "In the meantime, of course, we'll drop by the Demaris cabin to resolve the gender of this child. Easily done—important to be certain about such things."

William nodded, and his blank confusion melted at last to a knowing smile which he privately exchanged with Ronald.

"Look at the forest trimline here!" sang Dr. Howe. He waved his arms like a great conductor summoning brass and drums to action. "Absolutely devastating. All to be charted—a catastrophic marvel of nature."

But William was already on his way, and Ronald and Jennifer gently grasped the elbows of the senior scientist to guide him after. They gained the path and crossed the bridge, three wise men and a daughter of God, gone to seek the newborn child.

RETURN TO AMBER...
THE ONE *REAL* WORLD, OF WHICH ALL OTHERS, INCLUDING EARTH, ARE BUT SHADOWS

ROGER ZELAZNY

The Triumphant conclusion of the Amber novels

PRINCE OF CHAOS   75502-5/$4.99 US/$5.99 Can

The Classic Amber Series

NINE PRINCES IN AMBER   01430-0/$4.50 US/$5.50 Can
THE GUNS OF AVALON   00083-0/$4.99 US/$5.99 Can
SIGN OF THE UNICORN   00031-9/$4.99 US/$5.99 Can
THE HAND OF OBERON   01664-8/$4.99 US/$5.99 Can
THE COURTS OF CHAOS   47175-2/$4.99 US/$5.99 Can
BLOOD OF AMBER   89636-2/$4.99 US/$5.99 Can
TRUMPS OF DOOM   89635-4/$3.95 US/$4.95 Can
SIGN OF CHAOS   89637-0/$3.95 US/$4.95 Can
KNIGHT OF SHADOWS   75501-7/$3.95 US/$4.95 Can

Four Wondrous Stories
of Adventure and Courage by
B R I A N
J A C Q U E S

MOSSFLOWER
70828-0/$4.99 US

REDWALL
70827-2/$4.99 US

MATTIMEO
71530-9/$4.99 US

MARIEL of REDWALL
71922-3/$4.99 US